Mending Bodies

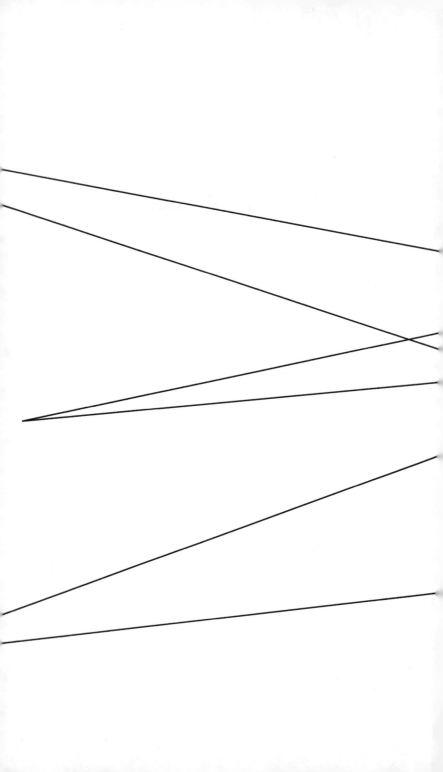

Mending Bodies

Hon Lai Chu

Translated from Chinese by Jacqueline Leung

TWO LINES
PRESS

Originally published in Chinese as 縫身
© 2010 Hon Lai Chu

Translation copyright © 2025 by Jacqueline Leung

Two Lines Press
www.twolinespress.com

ISBN: 978-1-949641-76-9
Ebook ISBN: 978-1-949641-77-6

Cover art: Radnatt via Getty Images
Cover design by Vivian Lopez Rowe
Typeset by Wengrow

Library of Congress Cataloging-in-Publication Data Available Upon
Request

Printed in the United States of America

This project is also supported in part by an award from the National
Endowment for the Arts.

A Meeting of Fish

I already knew they were at the door when the doorbell rang. It was an afternoon in plum rain season, lush mold blooming all around. May had always been punctual; I just hadn't thought the person she'd joined her body with would be the same.

"So, they're right on time," the man I was sewn to said, staring at the clock above our door, dismay seeping into his voice. He shifted, tugging at the wound connecting our chests. Because of May, he'd had to sacrifice his daytime sleep—it would have been impolite if one of us were unconscious when someone came all this way to visit.

It was less than a month into our own conjoining, and we'd already finished most of the sleeping pills our doctor had prescribed. Before going under the knife, he and I had agreed to take turns sleeping, so we would have space to get used to each other's bodies and still savor our time alone. And by sleeping at different hours, we could maybe even dream different dreams.

Handing over the bottle of brown pills, our doctor had said, "These will help you cope with the physical discomfort and any persistent, minor inflammation." He had broad, symmetrical shoulders and a body that was singular, whole, with no obvious signs of lacerations beneath his white coat and mask. I wondered then what a doctor so young, who hadn't been cleaved or cut open, could possibly know about conjoinment, but he spoke so authoritatively I felt guilty for doubting him.

True to his word, after we were discharged from the hospital, not a single moment passed without the stinging that felt like ants scurrying all over our skin. We writhed, attempting to arrange our limbs comfortably, and couldn't even move as we liked. But every time a conflict seemed imminent, one of us would swallow a brown pill, and in seconds, our exasperation would be washed away by lethargic sleep. This was why we never argued and never said words we later regretted. Whenever we spoke about this small triumph, we enjoyed a rare moment of happiness, something akin to pride.

We opened our door to May and a man standing in the dim corridor, holding a large basket of succulent green apples. The green reflected off their faces, making May's smile an eerie sort of friendly. I couldn't help but feel shocked, not by the ghastliness of their expressions, but the way their bodies clung together beneath a curious seam in their shirt, tucked away but still visible. It was enough for me to imagine their two different bodies, chests drilled and sewn together until their skin, muscles, cartilages, and tissues were connected as if by a small, short bridge. From now on, their bodies led only to one another.

After our surgery, we made sure to stay away from mirrors and glass of any kind. Whenever we showered or changed clothes, we lowered our eyes so we wouldn't catch the reflection of our flesh in the water or on the windows. We had gone to such lengths to avoid looking at the place where we were joined, only for our first visitors to ambush us with a glimpse of theirs as soon as we opened the door.

We shuffled aside to let them sidle through the narrow doorway. They went into the living room, sat down on the couch, and one of them said, "What a nice apartment."

By the time we served coffee, the rain was falling harder, hitting the windows and the city beyond like fistfuls of beans. The men got into a fervent discussion about the sound system we'd installed. May shifted closer and whispered in my ear. "Does it hurt?"

It was taboo to ask, but the way she looked when she said it reminded me of what now seemed so long ago, the days we'd spent huddled together in our university dorm, rolling cigarettes and prattling on about our professors, our classmates, and our dissertation writing that seemed to stretch on forever while rain crawled in tendrils down the foggy window of our room.

"I won't say it hurts." I lowered my voice, my words quickly drowned out by the pummeling rain. "I just feel each part of myself more acutely than before. My head, shoulders, chest, collarbones, abdomen, limbs, like an overweight backpack." I sorely missed the days before my surgery, when I was just a wisp of soul, so light I might vanish from this world once I crossed a road or slipped behind a building. But these were thoughts I kept to myself.

"More weight isn't necessarily bad," May said, glancing at her man. "We go further when we plant our feet firmly on the ground." Her gaze was unreadable—defensive or controlling, I couldn't tell.

They finished their coffee and stood to leave. We co-ordinated our heads to peer out the window, waving as May and her partner exited our building and reemerged on the street.

"They walk in perfect unison wherever they go," I said, embarrassed that we weren't able to do the same.

"Anyone can do that with some practice," he said dismissively. "It's just something people do to show off after being conjoined for a while."

I watched them disappear around the corner, feeling like something that had always been important to me was leaving forever. Suddenly, I remembered that May had told me her partner's name—Kui. I don't know how it was written, whether it meant someone who was tremendous or able or strong. I'd never had the chance to find out, and now he was an inseparable part of her.

By the time the man I was conjoined with dragged us to bed, he was utterly exhausted and heavy-eyed. I slept at midnight, so his bedtime started at noon. We never asked what the other person did while we were asleep. When the rain stopped, sunlight gleamed almost imperceptibly in the room and cast our shadow onto the white wall. I stared at the shape of us, scrutinizing our shadow's silhouette and shade, and tried to decipher to what it might have originally belonged. A tent, a strange hill, some prehistoric dinosaur? Then I looked at my pallid feet and my blue tights, his folded knee and plaid shirt, his long arm splayed across my stomach. For a moment everything felt distant, as if it all came from some other planet. I had no idea why I was trapped in a body like this.

It was not my decision, nor was it any individual's decision. The stage must have been set a long time ago, and we were simply bearing the collective responsibility. It was a logic that applied to conjoinment and many other matters of the world, like being born and becoming a person, a woman, a man.

I'd always thought I could avoid being tethered to these larger forces. Years ago, I was just like any other kid in the city, enjoying my transient freedom before I became an adult. Everything seemed to happen somewhere so far away, we could still live in our deluded fantasies. By the time we grew up and had no choice but to face them, maybe things were already irrevocably changed, and we were inevitably doomed.

When that time came, a certain sound engulfed me like an ocean, as if to drown me in its depths. It drew near, a distant rumble, like a train chugging along rusted tracks. I first heard it in the classroom whenever my attention strayed. Then, going home from school, the noise seemed to stream out of every open window on the street. I went inside the building my mother and I lived in, walking down the long, narrow corridor of apartments, and the whirring resounded from every unit, so loud I felt it would run me over.

I slid a key into the lock and opened the door. The apartment was filled with piles of plastic bags and bits of fabric. My mother sat in the center of the mess, her brows knit in concentration as she busily operated a sewing machine, where all the noise was coming from. The machine looked new and came with a pedal. It made quick work of a piece of white cloth, stitching a dash of red across the fabric in a matter of seconds.

Later that night at dinner, my mother looked at the pile of clothes she'd made and said, "Finally, some life and action in the city." It was her first day of work after a long spell of unemployment. When the city's factories had moved to cheaper places, she and many other seamstresses lost their stable jobs. But a week after the Conjoinment Act was announced, a hospital contracted her for a rush order of clothes for the first group of conjoined patients. She would be paid handsomely, nearly a full-time wage, as long as she delivered the clothes on time.

That same year, health professionals who had been

forced to retire early were brought back to their posts, and medical students who'd spent months looking for jobs were promptly hired. Car manufacturers that were in the red thrived with more pre-orders than they could handle as they released new models with seats for the conjoined. Interior designers, repairmen, architects, and construction workers found work once more with renovations, building wider entrances and hallways. Furniture factories on the brink of closure also hired new staff so they could make chairs, desks, toilets, bathtubs, and sinks by the thousands for their new conjoined customers.

"It's loud everywhere, so employment must be on the rise again." As she washed our dishes, my mother told me that before the slowdown, people had protested because of all the noise—screeching tires on the highway, ticking traffic lights, the digging and piling of construction sites, all that ineffable clamor from manufacturing, which exceeded an acceptable decibel level. They claimed that the noise affected their hearing, impeded their understanding of what other people were trying to say, and caused their mental health to deteriorate. But when the projects came to a halt, one after the other, people realized that piercing silence was even harder to bear.

On a talk show discussing the Conjoinment Act, a psychologist refuted the argument that the law was passed purely for economic reasons and said that society was in a state of crisis graver than ever before. The obsolete institution of marriage, racial conflict, wealth discrepancy, the many contrived wars—they all came from our inability to fill the existential lack we were born with as individuals.

"No person is complete on their own," he said. Society's current systems had failed to fill our emptiness. He doubled down when the host challenged him with the practical difficulties of conjoinment: "Only by being with another person can we experience the cycles of joy, heartbreak, harmony, and conflict necessary to arrive at true fulfillment."

The leader of the opposition party had also voiced his anxieties, though few understood him or paid attention. He said that conjoinment was an elaborate political ploy to make citizens forget about their long campaign for the city's independence. The government was introducing these measures so people would exhaust themselves struggling with the bodies of other people, leaving them too tired to care about matters of society. If the Conjoinment Act was passed, he said desperately, people would be in too much physical pain to go to protests.

Only environmentalists remained optimistic. One weighed in on the issue, laying out an idealistic blueprint for the future. She said, "A conjoined couple will shower, eat, and travel together, consuming less gas and water than if they were single. Also, fewer people will live alone, saving space and resources like furniture."

But for all these opinions, hardly anyone expressed their total agreement or disagreement. Only a long time later, when I stepped into adulthood, did I learn that a certain ambivalence toward policies we had no power over was the last effective resort for protecting our remaining freedoms. If we obeyed as if it didn't really matter, or carefully looked for the loopholes, we could secretly map the limits of their control.

Every evening after a day's work, my mother would ask me to put on the white shirts and pants she'd made and check them for flaws that may reduce her pay. I could only ever fill up half of every set. Sometimes she would leave the sleeves hanging or let the pantlegs drag across the floor, but other times she would squeeze in and support the fabric with her own body. When she did that, her eyes clouded over with an unreadable emotion, until she looked like someone completely unfamiliar to me.

As I tried on more clothes each day, the allowance

my mother gave me increased. Eventually I saved enough to buy a rectangular mirror to hang on my closet door. In the morning, as soon as I woke from my dreams, I would stand in front of the mirror to inspect my body for any tiny change, the same way my mother scrutinized her clothes. I bought outfits in every color, and all kinds of makeup—blushes, lipsticks, eyebrow pencils, powder, eyeliners. Every now and then I dolled myself up to try to become someone else, while my mother stood back and watched me with disapproval all over her face.

And then, the evening winter turned into spring, I looked into the mirror as my mother draped a shirt she'd just finished sewing over me. Something about the sight made us both start. Somehow, without us having noticed, I'd grown almost to the size of her clothes.

"Just a tiny bit more," my mother said, measuring the gap with her little finger.

"Am I bloated from the humidity?" I asked. She said nothing and stuck herself into the other half of the shirt. I looked at our reflection: we were like actors posing as a conjoined couple. But soon the gray hair on my mother's head, the wrinkles on her face, and the saggy skin around her neck became evident in the mirror, etched as if with a needle's tip. Her gaze clouded, and she was a stranger once again. I never knew if this meant she was disappointed about having exceeded the age for conjoinment surgery or if she was relieved to have no part to play in any of it. Later, I would also feel this listlessness as I faced my own ordeals. Everyone has an unspeakable struggle that is strictly their own, a burden that cannot be shared or lifted by others.

But I did understand why my mother looked so cold whenever she watched me inspect my skin and hair and as I picked out my clothes and shoes. She must have realized a long time ago that looks couldn't be relied upon. On Monday mornings, once she'd dropped off the clothes at the hospital, she would make up all sorts of excuses to wander the maze of corridors and areas off-limits to visitors, curiosity getting the better of her. She had seen so many beautiful men and women, with perfect, supple skin and lithe limbs and sinewy muscles, there for their special day—to get sliced open and then sewn together. On the operating table, those young men and women had no control over how their scars would look afterward. That depended entirely on their surgeon: if they were frustrated, calm, or bored that day, all of which dictated how the sutures healed.

"Even if they get a good surgeon, once a body is cut

open, the parts that remain intact will also slowly wilt, like flowers in a vase, vibrant but for a short time only," my mother said. I wished I could forget what she told me, but after that, I could no longer bring home flowers or foliage split from their stems or roots—they reminded me too much of the people on the streets and scared me so deeply.

"This won't do you any good in the long term," my mother always told me when she looked at my vanity table and my disheveled collection of bottles, filled with different colored powders and liquids.

But is anything wholly good? I wondered, and couldn't come up with an answer.

⌒

Before our conjoinment surgery, he and I put in an application to update our ID, agreeing to discard our old names for a new, shared one.

"It's not like anyone will talk to just you or me anymore," he said. "It's both of us or neither of us." I wasn't sure about that, but couldn't say why, which made me wonder if I had an opinion in the first place.

Once we got our new ID, I stored the card away in the back of a drawer. Like lots of people who can't recite their ID number off the top of their head, I found it hard to recall our new name. At events, whenever people asked me to introduce myself, my mind would go blank and I'd stagger into an awkward pause. Soon I grew fearful of names altogether, because after that short, discomforting pause, I was perpetually tempted to say my old name. I'd manage to hold my tongue, but it always reminded me of his old name and mine. We had completely different, unrelated names. If we hadn't said them out loud, hadn't decided to meet and get to know each other, we wouldn't have thought to join our bodies. By some chance occurrence, he'd approached me that one day and told me his name was Nok.

"Not 'Lok' as in happy but 'Nok' as in music, the sounds people use to numb their emotions," he explained. I didn't think to keep his name in my heart at the time. My mind was elsewhere, filled with other fanciful things. Yet change always starts from small, unidentified moments— by the time I realized just how critical this was, I was already a poor swimmer flailing in a maelstrom.

That day, he walked up to me and flashed the card with a number in his hand. I showed him mine and the mood lightened somewhat, as if the cards were a source of comfort, setting the parameters of our meeting.

We were surrounded by huge aquariums, with vibrant tropical fish all swimming in teh same direction. This was a newly opened Japanese restaurant. A server came to our table and gave us tea and menus. A long silence ensued, neither of us opening our mouths to speak until we saw a blue gourami suddenly give chase to a gold one. Then he said, "The water in these tanks flows with a strange rhythm."

We hadn't picked the restaurant or when we would meet. I hadn't chosen to dine with this man in front of me, but these were the conditions we accepted without complaint. Around a month before, we had each submitted an application to Magical Meets, a body-matching center. After we paid our fees, the center paired us up according to height, weight, skin color, age, and metabolic rate.

I'd signed up for the program with every intention to scorn it. In my dissertation workshop, Professor Foot once gave this advice: "If you're having trouble writing your paper and it feels like you need to weed out some thoughts, it's time to stop spacing out in front of the computer and *do* something."

"Do what?" someone asked.

"Make the fear that paralyzes you in your sleep real. Stand before it—don't turn away—and look. Record it if you can."

Which was why I ended up filling out a form from a body-matching ad and submitted my online application. But sitting in this chilly restaurant, I found myself unable to continue mocking the situation, and in fact felt more flustered than ever. I sipped my green tea, tasting its faint hint of rust, and realized my sense of satisfaction hadn't been coming from ridiculing the matching program, but from my mother's relief when I pretended to be interested, how she sighed and said, "You're finally considering conjoinment."

My doctor also commended the decision. "The younger you are when you undergo surgery, the less likely you'll reject your partner's body." Even the staff at the matching center sounded unusually hopeful over the phone. I was momentarily comforted by their encouragement, but as soon as I stopped to consider how I was feeling, dread settled in my heart.

Professor Foot didn't know I was meeting this man—I had never shared anything personal with him—and I was sure that by sitting in this restaurant, I was becoming the type of person he despised.

"Do you think the fish here feel trapped?" Nok asked. "Humiliated? With all these people eating their own kind in front of them?" He shoved some raw salmon into his mouth and made a face at the tank.

I turned my head and caught sight of a neon tetra twisting in and out of a piece of artificial coral obsessively, like it had no control over its body.

"Maybe their sight isn't good enough to see the dishes on the table. Maybe they don't understand what humans are doing," I said. "Or they could be used to the strong preying on the weak, in which case this dining area beyond the glass is just meaningless scenery.

"Most importantly," I added with finality, "we don't eat tropical fish." I bit into a dank piece of tuna.

"I hear medical students get together every day after school to eat raw meat until they feel completely indifferent to the blood. They do it to get over the unease of dissecting flesh so they can become outstanding surgeons."

I was holding my breath, arrested by the pulses of bubbles rising inside the tanks. At first, they were little more than small pockets of air, like insects chirring, but soon the vibrations grew wild, forcing their way toward us. Rather than the water, I probably should have tried to hear the meaning behind his words, everything he left unsaid, which seemed to pour into my eardrums along with the current.

"Do you plan to join your body with someone?" He

finally got straight to the point, no longer able to stand our silence.

"I'll need to cut off a part of myself, won't I?"

"Depends, conjoinment surgery has advanced a lot."

"I'm scared of blood and mangled bodies."

"You won't see a thing. You'll fall asleep as soon as the anesthetic is injected. By the time you wake, everything will be over."

"But I'll still feel the incision on my body. Some people's wounds never heal after their bodies are sewn together."

"Those are very rare cases, and there's a risk to everything. Say you remain a whole individual. Your unbroken skin could invite assault from those who are joined and jealous of your independence. Is there anyone who can guarantee that their body will stay intact forever?" He proceeded to note several recent trafficking cases involving human limbs and organs, terrifying stories that happened around us every day. It was just that, as the fortunate and unaffected, we feigned ignorance to keep ourselves happy and to feel secure.

The smallest fish in the tank, swimming among the bed of water plants and glass pebbles, was hardly larger than a speck of dust and never came across another fish its own size. I pointed at it and said, "Do you think that fish will get eaten by a larger fish before it grows up?"

Skeptical, he asked, "Is that fish a pet or pet food?"

After I left the restaurant, I forgot almost everything about Nok. His face, his scent, what he said—it was as if I had never met him. Only a few feeble tropical fish writhed out of the murky tank and breached my mind. They kept me awake that night, so I turned on my laptop and started working on the dissertation outline I was supposed to have handed in more than a month before. I wrote without stopping, the fish in close pursuit behind me. After typing out the last sentence, I lifted my head and looked out at the sky. It was a wide expanse of gray, the underbelly of a fish swimming high over me.

Outline, Part I

Topic: Third Identities and Hidden Selves—the Faces of Conjoinment

Abstract: This study examines the origins of conjoinment, from the earliest representations of conjoined human beings in mythology, legends, and folklore to changes in their social status over time. Through these perspectives, the paper explores the shadow that still exists between two bodies when they are connected, how it flourishes and expands, and whether it is capable of birthing new selves.

I. A Crack in the Consciousness

In existing literature, the first verified conjoined creature was not human, but fish. The fish inhabited a pond in a rural village in northern India and has been named

Parineeta by modern teratologists researching conjoined embryos. An unknown species, it was golden and had one body, one head, and two faces, which classified it as a diprosopus, a condition more often found in cows and sheep. If this occurs in a human embryo, the embryo will likely perish in the womb before it gets to maturity.

In his book *On Culture and Monsters*, the academic David Lynch raises the case of Parineeta as a study of how people express their fear and fascination with biological anomalies. In the spring of 380 AD, Parineeta was swimming leisurely in the pond, unaware that the moment that would alter the course of its fate and the entire study of conjoinment had quietly arrived. Karan, an eight-year-old boy, was kneeling by the bank and had been staring at Parineeta for most of the day. Finally, he ran back home to tell his mother; as soon as the mother heard about the strange sight, she abandoned her apron and cooking—the food still simmering in the pot—and hurried to the pond to see for herself. In no time, their neighbors, family, friends, everyone who was curious, gathered to peer at Parineeta's faces, murmuring among themselves as they wondered if it was the prank of a child or if that deformed fish had fallen right from the sky. For a short while, Parineeta's existence excited the peaceful village like a carnival. Every afternoon, whenever villagers had a break from work, they would go to the pond to visit this extraordinary fish, throwing food and coins into the water to make wishes and ill confessions they had so far kept to themselves.

However, this period of happiness was short-lived, and soon Parineeta's reproductive capabilities led to its demise. When the villagers saw that more and more diprosopic fish were being born in the water, any excitement they had was replaced by worry. The oldest woman in the village declared, "This is an omen of unprecedented catastrophe." So the villagers tried to come up with ways to exterminate the fish. They were afraid that eating the meat would pass diprosopic genes to their children, and that burning or burying them would invite the wrath of evil spirits. At last, they decided to capture five giant, carnivorous tortoises, which they took to be symbols of good fortune, and released them into the pond. Not only did the giant tortoises resolve the disaster, but the massacre in the water was also a show that entertained the bored villagers.

In Lynch's view, the appearance of the diprosopic fish provided the villagers with a spectacular impetus to bond amid crisis. A community strengthens and becomes more cohesive when adversaries exist, which is why "monsters," representing the forces of all evil, have played such an indispensable role in the development of societies across the ages. And so it may have been good for the village that, after the elation they got from ridding themselves of the diprosopic fish, they proceeded to exterminate all the conjoined children and their mothers.

In the year 1109, in a small town fifty kilometers from Parineeta's village, a young woman named Priyanka Johar gave birth to male twins joined at the head. After the midwife extracted the twins from the mother's body, the first words she said were, "Devils! Is this punishment from the gods?"

Priyanka only stared at her children, speechless and in tears. The town elders took this as a sign that the gods had been angered—only sinful women birthed mutant children. Thus, they made a severe decision. To save the townspeople from divine rage, they must burn Priyanka and her sons as offerings before the blood dried and hardened on their skin. Weak from childbirth, Priyanka did not resist and only begged the person carrying her to the sacrificial site, her closest friend in the town, to hurry in putting her on the fire. She must be ashes by the time her husband returned; after all, he loathed the stench of human blood. Lynch's book made no mention of the husband's response to the deaths of his wife and children, only that he married another woman from the same town sixty days later. They had eight children, all of whom had normal bodies.

Much later, sixteenth-century priests and doctors made up all sorts of reasons why Priyanka Johar ended up with conjoined twins. She could have eaten food unsuited for pregnancy, seen too much grotesque art, drunk polluted cow's milk, sat with poor posture, or it was possibly the result of the spite of the animals her husband brought home as a hunter. But most were inclined to attribute it to the atrocious imagination of a pregnant woman and her incessant fancies and dreams. Lynch was not interested in any of this; he was eager instead to understand why Priyanka had simply accepted the sin her senseless elders had imposed on her. He writes, "Priyanka Johar sided with the villagers, believing that she had been seized by evil, and that her spirit could only be cleansed by the immolation of her body. She was the one who pushed her children and herself to a place of absolute solitude."

However, Lynch's research failed to take into account the context in which these incidents happened, time and place also being fateful factors affecting the trajectory of people's lives. Long before that first diprosopic fish was recorded, conjoinment was already iconic in our visual tradition. In Roman mythology, Janus is a god who looks simultaneously in front of and behind him, the future and the past, with his two faces. Oannes, a Greek water god with a fish's body, human legs, and two heads—one fish and one man—emerged from the waves to impart science, art, and law to early civilization. He taught humans about planting and foraging, and slipped back into the depths of the sea as soon as he had shared his wisdom. In modern medicine, Janus and Oannes would both be classified as diprosopi. Are conjoined beings then divine retribution or sources of knowledge or both? If Priyanka's children were born in England and not India, would they have lived like the Biddenden Maids, Mary and Eliza Chulkhurst of Kent? Joined at the hip, the sisters were a pygopagus. They fulfilled people's predatory curiosity toward aberrations and helped thousands of philanthropists fulfill their need to show off their altruism. Aside from their anatomy, they were famous for their inexplicable selflessness to be with each other until death. When Mary took ill and passed away at the age of thirty-four, the doctor suggested surgical separation to Eliza to save her life, but Eliza refused and said, "As we came together we will also go together." (The frequent arguments, fights, and anxiety of being trapped in a joined body never seemed to apply to them at all.)

Their deaths helped the church receive a donation of twenty acres of land. Every Sunday, it distributed bread and cakes branded with the sisters' faces to feed the poor and the hungry.

In *Half: Our Conjoined Future*, Martin Stewart writes, "In every person's heart is a dark place that even they cannot reach. There, a mirror reflects their entire consciousness, which is but a piece of the puzzle. By gathering all these little pieces, we get to envision the world." These academics believe that everything in the world exists first and foremost in the human mind—like myths, sprung from the imagination of the ancient Greeks—before it becomes tangible. If disasters and blessings can be derived from the same origin, then, in an abstract sense, they are also conjoined. Fear has a primordial place in our equanimous lives, and that is the purpose conjoined people exist to fulfill.

Solo

The clock read six-thirty. It was Wednesday, first class at eight-thirty, with Professor Foot. I changed my clothes, printed out my dissertation outline, and took the train to the university with many other sleep-deprived students.

Those who signed up for Professor Foot's course knew that his classes never actually started at eight-thirty. From the early morning, cigarette smoke lingered amid the trees and beside the swimming pool, rounded the stairs, and drifted down the stone steps outside the library, spreading until every part of the campus was suffused, a faint smell inhaled into the tracheae and lungs of every person. Half an hour before class officially began, the scent led us to Professor Foot like an unspoken code we shared. Sometimes, we found his silhouette standing by a tree or caught him looking at his reflection in the water. Other times, he was sitting in the bushes with stray cats as they slept. Once he saw that we had arrived, he would give us a wave, then take hand-rolled cigarettes from his pocket and distribute them to the crowd of students. We'd flick our lighters, taking drag after drag of acrid smoke.

All the students here knew. As we talked nonsense—speaking to one another or to ourselves, letting out yells for no reason, or mimicking how we each held our cigarettes—class had already begun. More times than we could count, before we'd even smoked through half of the stash, the security guard would come up to Professor Foot with a smile on his face and say, in a tone reserved for habitual troublemakers, "The campus is a smoke-free area." Professor Foot's answer was always the same. He would take a pull, point at his empty left pantleg and cane, and say there wasn't a moment when he wasn't agonized by his wound, and the cigarettes he rolled himself were the only things that offered a brief, numbing respite. Then he would gesture toward us. "Tobacco helps them think too; it stimulates their nerves." Neither the security guard nor the professor was convinced by the exchange, though it was the security guard who always retreated, not keen to argue, pretending he'd never seen the people puffing away.

For most of us, we probably weren't addicted to to-bacco. We weren't drawn by the smoking, but by a false sense of finding people just like ourselves. There was a certain atmosphere with the group coming together for a smoke in the morning that made us feel like we had within our grasp a common language, which allowed us to accept others and be accepted in turn. The smoke we exhaled swirled and rose, condensing into a dark cloud, an umbrella over our heads, giving us a place to stay.

We never quite pinpointed why we found Professor Foot so charismatic. If not for his pocketfuls of cigarettes, it must have been his left leg, amputated below the knee, or his manner of speech. All we knew was that, even if it was one of those eight-thirty classes we all loathed so much, there would be no empty seats in the hall as long as it was Professor Foot standing at the lectern.

⌣

"Doesn't anyone sleep around here, all of you showing up so bright and early?" Professor Foot couldn't help but groan once he walked in and saw the dark mass of heads filling up the hall on the first lecture of the term. "How am I going to mark all the final papers with so many of you?" Later, once we got to know him better, we would learn that this was just how he expressed himself. But no one understood him at the time, and unease rippled through the room.

"So, what brings you here?" He swept his gaze across the faces in the crowd, looking each of us in the eye as we gave no response. "To watch a middle-aged man drag his one leg onstage?"

Still no sound but the whirring of the air conditioning. He laughed, a loud squawk from the back of his throat that reminded me of crows screeching as they circled the hills. He stopped, and then he said, "Do you know what universities produce in droves each year?"

The lecture hall was becoming uncomfortable with how quiet it was. Professor Foot let the pause drag on before he finally broke the silence. "A handful of geezers who yap nonstop but have no idea what they're talking about, and countless dumb kids who don't know how to speak up."

He sighed. "Those who want to leave can leave. You're welcome to. As I said, the number of students in this room is abhorrent. You'd be doing all of us a favor if you volunteered to go."

The hall was large, but no one moved a muscle or so much as shifted a foot, as if we were built into the room like the tables and chairs.

"You need me to be nastier. I can do that."

He divided the hall into four for group discussions and made us appoint representatives to present to the rest of the class. The topic: "The Necessity of Disability in Society." I've completely forgotten what we talked about and what the material was, only that when class was about to end, Professor Foot pulled out a handkerchief and wiped the sweat off of his forehead, huffing as he said, "Thank Christ, that's one lesson done." But for the rest of us, the air conditioning had been so cold, we were shivering the whole time.

From that day onward, we never moved from that topic. It leached into our university lives along with the professor's distinctive footsteps, the nicotine stains lining his fingernails and teeth, and his assignments and jokes. Students who liked his lectures dragged him out of his office under the pretense of having questions about class so they could take him for lunch or afternoon tea at the open-air café, and slowly a group formed. When we deliberately forgot his last name and gave him the nickname "Foot," it brought us so much joy, because we thought we'd distinguished ourselves from the obscure mass of students in the class and formed a special relationship with him.

Often, when we ate together, our conversations revolved around Professor Foot's amputated leg. Sitting with us, he wasn't bothered in the slightest, and even told us why he was adamant about not getting a prosthetic.

"That contraption will only erode my bones and muscles. More importantly, trying to hide the fact that I have only one leg is such a futile and meaningless thing to do."

We'd chatter animatedly and endlessly about his missing limb. Somehow, the sparks for these debates were only ever kindled whenever we ate and drank together. Someone pointed out that government-funded institutions like universities always reserved employment quotas for the disabled. As long as one was willing to make their disability public and show it off in an interview, it wouldn't be difficult for someone like Professor Foot to secure a professorship. His missing limb was therefore an asset to his livelihood.

Another student thought that the professor had sacrificed a perfectly good leg to get conjoined, but after a few years, he inexplicably went under the knife again to regain his mobility. Yet another student interjected by saying it was a way for the professor to retain his independence and integrity. With his leg missing, he was neither a whole person nor part of a conjoined pair, which saved him from having to choose between the two states of existence, and he could also abstain from all the politics advocating for either conjoinment or physical independence that actually harbored secret agendas. The whole time we talked, Professor Foot sat quietly, not admitting but also not denying the speculations and claims we were making about his body, and he only smiled unassumingly as he set his eyes on our faces one by one.

We laughed boisterously, raising even more nonsensical theories, and made brazen fun of the professor, subjecting him to our fantasies even though he was right in front of us. I sat with the group, not saying anything but enjoying the senseless banter, until I happened to meet Professor Foot's eyes, looked deep into their recesses, and found the mockery in them to be so penetrating, they pierced my nerves. Unlike most people when ridiculed, the professor was hardly embarrassed or resigned; he'd kept his silence and had been looking down on us this entire time. When the group laughed, he laughed too, as though the people sitting in front of him were nothing but fools.

But in spite of all this, I still wanted him to be my dissertation advisor, perhaps for the same reason most of the class wanted him to supervise their research. It wasn't because we were especially diligent with our studies or zealous about a particular topic. We just thought he could help us write a unique sort of paper that would lead us to an exit path or opening, something that might ease our anxiety about our imminent entry into the workforce.

On the day of the interviews for selecting dissertation students, I stepped into his office and sat down in the chair across from him. We were the only ones in the oddly stuffy room.

"Who are you?" he asked.

A little reluctantly, I told him my name and year.

"No, you're someone who doesn't smile," he said, staring right at me.

"Oh? Why should I smile? It's not like I'm here to sell my smiles."

"Don't you know? Our mouths are like doors to a house. If you don't show that you're welcoming, how can other people work up the courage to approach you? Not only must you smile a lot, you must also learn the right kind of smile at the right time."

"Just because someone's smiling doesn't mean they're pleasant or friendly."

"Who said smiles are friendly and kind? Smiling is polite, a greeting, the most basic social skill." He looked more shocked than I was. "You're already in your third year, and you still haven't learned such a simple thing?" he mumbled, as if he didn't mean for anyone to hear what he said.

◡

The day after my Magical Meets date, I could barely concentrate in class. I read my dissertation outline over and over, mulling what kind of facial expression I should put on for my consultation with the professor after the lecture.

His office was at the very end of the corridor. As you walked toward it, you could hear the drag of your steps against the carpet, the strange sound of your body weight. I wore ballet flats on purpose to lessen the friction between my heels and the floor. Each office had a wooden door with a square window that allowed people to look in and see the professors and tutors at work, heads lowered over their desks, but Professor Foot always hung things over the glass to stop people from peeking. Sometimes it was a mirror, sometimes a soup bowl, but most often he taped up newspaper clippings. This time, it was an article about a controversial art installation in Hungary. The artist had displayed a rotting cow carcass in the exhibition space, attracting swarms of feeding flies.

I knocked on the door and went in, looking at his back, which was twitching slightly as he clacked away on his computer. He must have heard my footsteps, but he didn't turn around.

"I finished my dissertation outline," I said loudly to his back.

"Are you proposing a topic on smiling?" He finally stopped typing and gazed through the only window in his office that led outside.

"No," I said.

"Do you know the point of a dissertation?" he asked. I followed his line of vision and saw a low tree, its leaves turning amber as the season changed, but I didn't know the name of that kind of tree.

"The point is to find an issue." He settled in to a long pause before continuing. "An issue that has always troubled you and keeps you from living a satisfied life. There are people who spend their whole lives plagued by problems they can't articulate until they lose their minds. Many never finish their papers. Many more never even start, and eventually some end up taking their own lives."

I stared at his profile. My face was stiff, unsure of what expression to wear.

He burst into abrupt laughter. He laughed hard, guffaws racking his entire body as if it were a hill splitting apart in an earthquake. When he finally calmed down, he said, his voice light as a twist of smoke in the air, "This is a joke."

He turned toward me, then he made a move to pull up his left pantleg. "Do you want to see my injury?"

I shook my head, gazing at a sleek, black crow perched on the telephone pole beside the tree, admiring the harmonious form of its head, wings, and claws. "It's just a wound, nothing special about that," I said.

⌒

After that uneventful consultation, an unspeakable change started to happen within my body. An inscrutable hormonal imbalance, or possibly the sudden fluctuation of some substance. Ever since that day, the temperature of the air conditioning in Professor Foot's office, the sun beaming outside the window, his desk strewn with newspaper clippings, the scent of his hair, the glide of the crow's flight—they lingered in my head, occupying every corner of my mind until not a bit of space was left.

Finally, I couldn't stand it any longer and wrote an

email to the professor. In my email, I had a sentence that read, *The premise of my paper is inspired by an experiment you led me to start.*

His response was short. *Then, you should keep experimenting until you finish.* I read it again and again, trying to decipher its meaning in different ways.

⌣

"Fieldwork puts a researcher's courage to the test—how much uncertainty and how much danger they're willing to throw themselves into." We were in his dusty car. He was driving while explaining why I should do fieldwork or employ similar methodologies to develop the direction of my paper.

"Are you scared?" he asked. The car left the university campus and sped along the highway. There were hardly any vehicles in the adjacent lanes. We traveled past a harbor of fluttering waves, then entered a dark and narrow tunnel, two rows of fluorescent lights receding endlessly on the ceiling. By the time we emerged, we were under a different sky. I couldn't name the place we were in. The trees, shops, gas stations, bus stops, and pedestrians all came together in an unfamiliar way, but I wasn't apprehensive in the slightest. I was in a car, sealed within its glass windows and locked doors, and that made me feel like I was simply inside the vehicle no matter where it took me.

"I'm no less afraid than you are." He drove us into a back alley with rugged pavement, where the walls were black and the gates pulled down. "You don't know where you're going, and as the one guiding it, I don't know what consequences the experiment will bring. Once people meet and touch, they slip into a desolate wasteland," he said before he parked the car.

We got out and stepped into a rundown hotel. The building looked like a black box with round, evenly spaced windows on the sides. The porter at the reception took a long look at us, then picked up a key card and led us to the elevator and up to our room without a word. At this point, I was still tranquil, as if drifting along the bottom of the sea. "No matter what building you're in, you're only inside the shell of your body," I told myself, feeling so acutely the beat of my heart, the tickle of my hair on my cheek, the painful scrape of my boots against the insteps of my feet; then we stepped into a spacious room. The room had a round window, and beyond the window was a beach that led to rolling white water.

The porter closed the curtains with an impassive face and left us alone. I seemed to know what was going to happen. I was taken aback by how unsurprised I was, the fear I'd been waiting for never arriving. At a loss, I wondered if I should feel sorry for myself for not being ignorant enough.

"In places like these, where no one wants to be remembered or identified, silence is the best hospitality. It makes guests feel right at home," Professor Foot said. I latched onto his words to distract myself. Then I stepped into the bathroom, turned on the faucet, and rinsed every secret part of my body thoroughly with soap.

After I slipped into the white sheets to cover myself, he also went to shower, the drone of the running water making it seem like an austere ritual, a task we were about to undertake with the mindset of participating in a tutorial or research presentation.

He lay beside me, sticky moisture filling the air between us. "To study the conjoined, you must first simulate being one of them, to live as they do and experience their problems, but you must also remain calm and objective to record and analyze the data." He explained the goal of the experiment like it was part of a lecture.

"Choosing a body compatible with yours is a laborious

affair." We began to act out the selection of a conjoinment partner. It was an elaborate process, but Professor Foot seemed to know just what to do. He put his ear against my chest to listen to my heartbeat, then we stood shoulder to shoulder in front of the mirror and measured our difference in height. Professor Foot was shorter than the average man, and without the padding of his clothes and shoes, his ribs were pronounced, making him look even more slight than he did in the lecture hall.

He took out a hemp rope from the drawer and tied my right leg to the half of his left leg. "We're going to pretend that we're conjoined. Now, we have three legs between us," he said. We placed our hands on each other's shoulders and tried to go from one end of the room to the other. But the room that had seemed spacious turned out to be full of hazards—chairs, slippers, wastebasket, coffee table, the carpet, all of which could easily trip us. We grew so exhausted, we had to catch our breaths on the bed. He untied the rope and we took turns lying on top, feeling how heavy the other person was to see if it was a weight we could bear.

"These are all important considerations when choosing someone. Who knows what kind of domestic accident might happen after your bodies are sewn together?"

He said that after the Conjoinment Act was passed, for a while, there was a huge surge in bookings for budget hotel rooms because people who knew they had to succumb to a conjoined life wanted to temporarily forget the turmoil of the outside world behind closed doors.

"Some decided to carefully examine the bodies that would soon become a part of them. Others weren't preparing for conjoinment, but as soon as conjoinment became a palpable future, they were desperate to meet the person they'd always wanted, and to leave traces on each other's bodies." He took out a cigarette from the pocket of his suit jacket and lit it.

"Don't doctors and the authorities decide which bodies we match with?" I couldn't quite believe what he was saying.

"Did you enjoy what we've done in this hotel?" As he spoke, the smoke he exhaled ribboned endlessly like it was being pulled.

"Does whether or not I liked it matter once it's already done?" I stared at the beach beyond the window, watching the waves slap against the shore with a certain rhythm. We were between tides, the sky already a little dark.

"Your immediate perception of your experience here is crucial, especially in a place like this. If people come to this hotel room not to satisfy some urgent need to do with conjoinment or reproduction or for some other exchange of benefit, but just because, then this room is an escape, a place for the rebellious to rest a while."

"How can you know what everyone who comes here is thinking? You're just speculating," I said.

He didn't respond to my question but told me that a pinhole camera had been installed in a surreptitious corner of the room where it wouldn't be discovered, and that it wasn't malicious. The camera was to record the interactions between guests, their gestures and facial expressions, to give researchers some fresh perspective.

"The camera captures more candor than words." So Professor Foot justified the voyeurism, and it felt like some part of me had been stabbed, as if I'd accidentally stepped on air in the dark and fallen into a trap. My only choice was to withdraw, to retreat within the perimeter of my body, and there, sleep overtook my consciousness. In my dream, I was riding in an elevator with no lights on. I was pushing the buttons to different floors. The doors opened and closed, but they only led to the same pitch-black corridor, never stopping at the floor I wanted to reach.

When I woke, Professor Foot was no longer in the room. The only thing he left was a note on the table with a skewed drawing of a map showing the way from the hotel to a nearby bus stop, where I could take a direct line back to campus.

⌣

Light was spilling through a crevice in the clouds by the time I got back to the dormitory. The day had just risen, a crow's cry piercing the air, tires gritted raw on the asphalt. I opened the door to our room and saw May sitting in front of her computer hugging her knees, the light of the monitor shining on her face. I could tell that she hadn't slept the entire night.

"Where did you go?" she asked, turning her head to look at me.

"My dissertation consultation." I lay on my bed and stared at the ceiling I was so familiar with, only to find it covered in cobwebs.

"Professor Foot is a workaholic who never sleeps." She gave a dry laugh.

"Are you also struggling with your paper?" I squinted at her screen, the text tiny as insects.

"I'm just thinking."

"About what?"

"The future."

"That's not something we can deal with now." I turned away, remembering that I'd yet to brush my teeth.

"All the more reason to plan."

"What have you got then?"

"Like, what kind of job I should get after graduation, even though that may not be up to me to decide. Who can guarantee that we won't end up unemployed? Or, more importantly, who will we spend our lives with? Conjoined people always get priority for jobs."

For a moment, I thought that she'd forgotten about the promise we'd made, but then I came to my senses and understood that she was trying to revoke it—a sign that change was already quietly taking place between us.

On the day we moved into the dormitory, May and I were assigned to the same room. Once we finished cleaning and unpacking our belongings, we started a long conversation that went from exam stress, fashion, lovers, and mothers to our schoolmates from orientation camp. We talked about all sorts of things. The more we spoke, the more we discovered points of view we hadn't thought of ourselves. They hatched like new cells inside our bodies, bringing us indescribable joy. Even when our conversation was put on hold by sleep, class, reading, or the other trivial matters of life, it would continue naturally once we reunited in our room, never running dry.

We used to say that when we graduated and had no choice but to leave our dormitory, we would move to the suburbs and rent an apartment together. The apartment would have a view of the bird sanctuary, and it would be a decision we shared, something that would give us the strength to get through life—or so we thought at the time.

"If you connect your body and share blood with someone who already has a stable job, their employer has to hire you as a conjoined spouse to comply with government legislation. We all know that, but doesn't that deprive people who reject conjoinment or are ineligible for the surgery of job opportunities? We're being groomed to become part of a dominant population that pushes others to the periphery of our society." May was reading a chapter of *Madness and Civilization* and was so indignant that she threw the book on the floor.

I had an urge to tell May about my aunt Myrtle, who was conjoined for over ten years but insisted on splitting from her partner by undergoing separation surgery and had lived without her left arm ever since. I was never able to tell anyone how much I adored and missed my aunt; my mother loathed the very mention of her and strictly forbade me from talking about her to anyone. "Your aunt is a deviant," she cautioned.

I never did tell May about Aunt Myrtle, and only suggested that we participate in the campaign to support body independence. "Even in a perilous world full of thorns, we can face anything as long as we have each other's backs," I said to her. For so long, I was captivated by the vision of us standing back to back and supporting each other—until I saw a picture of rachipagus twins in the book *An Introduction to the Conjoined*. I stared at the twins, at the joined flesh of their backs, and was shocked by what I had imagined.

It was also possible that our resistance to conjoinment was merely to preserve our physical independence, an attempt to save something already on the verge of ruin. One afternoon, when we were shopping in a large chain furniture store, a beige lace curtain happened to catch both our eyes, and from that moment onward, a whole new way of life unfolded for us.

"These curtains would totally change the ambiance of our room," I told May. We were surrounded by many other curtains of different colors and textures.

"We can do whatever we want and no one will see," she said, a similar sentiment stirring within her. We took the curtains back to our room and hung them over our bare glass window, shielding our space from sunlight and sightlines from the windows of the dorm opposite our building. Although we'd long stopped caring about prying eyes—after all, we'd also spent many brain-fogged afternoons perched by our own window, looking through many other windows to see what people did in their rooms— once we closed our new curtains, the snug darkness of our interior made us giddy with excitement.

By then, we had been living in the dorm for several months. Free from the control of our families, we lived our nights like days and days like nights. We stayed silent when we didn't want to speak and let our faces fall blank when we wished to be left alone. We only ate delicious food with no care for nutrition and smoked whenever we wanted. But still there had been something lacking that we couldn't quite put our finger on, until we stood in our space behind closed doors and drawn curtains, and—I forget who did it first—started taking off our sweaters, coats, blouses, skirts, socks, underwear, and bras. We sat at our desks and worked, read a book, drank tea, and tidied our notes as usual. That was the moment when we realized that people weren't bound by the gaze and criticism of others, but the habits we had normalized ourselves. From then on, we stripped every time we returned to our room, letting our skin come into contact with the dust in the air, knowing we wouldn't get sick as long as we kept our space clean and set the air conditioning at a comfortable temperature.

I took those times for granted and thought we would go on like that forever; only now, May was pointing out the dead end we were headed toward. Once again, I felt I was stabbed in some extremely fragile part of me, so I buried my face in the cleft of my pillows, into that soft chasm. Vaguely, I heard May's voice as she said, "Life isn't as abundant and free as we wish it to be."

⌒

When I opened my eyes, the room was as dim as a bygone dream. May was nowhere to be seen, and her computer was turned off. A bird's cry echoed like a choked sob from far away. I paused, stunned by the sound, then I felt that the bird was only missing a listener for its woes. I got out of bed and drew back the curtains but couldn't see any sign of the bird; there was nothing outside but buildings and a cloudless sky. A note had been placed on top of a book on my desk: 8:30. *Foot. Guest. Attendance.* It was in

May's handwriting, sharing a cryptic message only I could decipher, a reminder for me to go to the important lecture we'd both said we would attend. At the start of the course, when we first received our syllabus, we made a commitment to each other to not miss this class.

Professor Foot told us he would start inviting guest speakers to our lectures toward the middle of the semester. The guests would have physical traits so incompatible with the urban landscape that they crashed and bled wherever they went, and we would get to hear from them in person.

"Through their experiences, you'll notice how cramped the seats can be, how low the ceilings. Our clothes and food portions are too small, and elevators hold too little weight—these are all things we've gotten used to, so we never notice that anything is wrong."

An imperious smile spread across his face as he taught us that even people walking down the same street were in distinct worlds of their own, and that the guest speakers he'd invited understood this more acutely because their bodies were markedly different. Once they set foot outside their homes, the inadvertent hostility of their surroundings might as well have been durians ready to drop from the trees without warning. None of us lived in the same world, and so we were all sojourners in our shared spaces.

"You think it's true that we can never find someone who lives in the same world as us?" I whispered to May, who was sitting next to me.

"Never." She shook her head, and in that moment, the sharp angle of her nose looked even more pronounced. "Everyone lives in their own world, but to avoid conflict, we fake companionship as if we're all kindred spirits."

"But if we've already made up our minds before we start, we'll never learn anything new," I retorted.

And so May and I promised to attend the lectures together, but with different goals in mind: she was there to prove her own thesis, and I was there to find fault in her argument and break it down.

◡

By the time this forsaken dream came back to me, it had amassed so much energy that it felt thicker than life, as though it were an event that had actually taken place, a memory I couldn't just push from my mind. In the dream, a man stood, slouching like an angler, like lots of people who couldn't straighten their limbs in this city. I knew his name was Bak, even though he'd never said it out loud. Bak stood looking at a wall. On the wall was a faded mural, and in a part where the color was peeling away, there was a trembling line of writing that read: *I am not me. Ching, December 10.* Beyond the wall was an empty construction site where a building had just been razed to the ground. That was where Ching, a fifteen-year-old boy, lived by himself after his parents left home, one then the other. He didn't go to school, didn't work, and had no relatives or friends. Officers from the urban renewal department paid him multiple visits to explain the compensation he would get if he complied with the eviction, but the boy was obstinate, and every time he just said, "I don't understand, I can't understand." Finally, he was the only resident left in the building. An officer from the department commented on the situation once by saying, "At that age, children are as much trouble as beasts."

A week before the building was to be pulled down, Ching ran to the playground and scribbled his last words on the wall. Then he went back home, a unit on the twenty-sixth floor, and jumped through the window. By the time he hit the ground, his body was twisted in bizarre angles.

Bak hopped the fence the developer had set up to look at the wall.

Winter came, and on a freezing cold night, Bak went for hotpot with a group of friends. But even after finishing all the food, they were still unbearably hungry.

"Maybe we didn't order enough meat," one of his friends said.

"It's like we've eaten nothing but air," said another.

"This isn't a hunger that food can satiate," Bak blurted out, then he led the group from the restaurant to the construction site, by now changed beyond recognition, to look at the wall. They stood there until their faces ached from the frigid wind, before someone suggested that they each leave something on the wall. They silently made their marks in the dark, and without even saying goodbye, the group went their separate ways.

Bak stood looking at the wall. The new building was already constructed up to the seventh floor, but the wall remained where it was. The only difference was that it had been eroded by wind and rain, and so a large part of its surface had fallen off, leaving an indentation in the shape of some nameless island.

⌣

The walk from the dormitory to the park beside the

library was just long enough for me to recall that dream, to retrieve its fragments and fill the gaps between them. As I got closer, I saw students huddled back to back, shadows of dense indigo like the reflection of a great, dark cloud in the sky, or maybe it was just so many people inhaling and exhaling smoke at the same time. Ahead of the scheduled guest speaker, Professor Foot had shared his photography on the university intranet, asking us to study the images, even reminding us several times.

"Look carefully at the photos he took, let them into your heart, and then forget them. Forgetting is as important as meticulous attention." He proceeded to lay down several house rules. "Class will continue for however long it takes for us to smoke all these cigarettes." The smile he gave was devious. "Everyone will get cigarettes from me, and like every Wednesday, class is dismissed the moment I run out. If you don't want to show up, no need to force yourself; don't waste my time or my cigarettes."

I stepped into the smother and sat down with my back to the crowd. Not long after, a classmate passed me a cigarette. I had just taken my first drag when I spotted the man in the middle of the circle. Although neither his face nor his body looked like Bak's in my dream, I was sure that he was Bak from the way he smoked, only he'd come in a different form, in a different time. Bak was talking about something that I suspected hadn't actually happened, but then I thought how even if everything we were told in class was a blatant lie, it wouldn't have much impact on our education.

"After the boy was buried, his older sister led me into his room. At first, they were planning on finding a house-keeper to clean up his belongings, but their father vehe-mently refused. He was afraid that someone who didn't know his son would steal the things he'd left behind and sell them," Bak said, adding that, in the sister's opinion, her father just didn't want a professional cleaner to erase the traces of his son, as though he'd never been born.

"Later, they decided to lock the room so no one could go in. But even through the door, they could still feel the brother's presence and hear his footsteps and the sighs that filled every corner of the space.

"His sister said to me, to reopen the door, they needed a reason. So they asked me to photograph every object in the room while they figured out what to do with them. I don't know their true intentions, maybe the father was hoping I would capture the spirit of his son, or the sister wanted me to help preserve some evidence of him, but it's not important. When I opened the door, I found that the light, temperature, and aura of the room didn't seem to be of this world—not of the living or the dead, but a bridge between two ends. The person living in that room had passed away, and the space he left behind was ambiguous and incomprehensible."

With a voice that sounded like it was rarely used, Bak said the boy had spent most of his time drawing, even though he never publicized his work. All he drew were young girls who he may have thought of as younger sisters. Other than his father and his older sister, he didn't have any family or friends he could talk to.

We quickly smoked through the cigarettes. It was the shortest class I could remember. In no time, the sun was right above our heads, or maybe our skin was too weak to stand the burn for very long. Students started standing up to leave and dispersed in every direction. I also stood up, but before I left, I turned my head to look at the broken circle of people. Bak was wrapped in the middle, his head and shoulders towering over the crowd like a range of hills.

After I returned to the dormitory, a small, black mark appeared in my vision and refused to go away no matter where I looked, scarring the room I was so familiar with, the streets, the sky, and people's faces with a persistent tear. When the mark finally faded, I logged on to the intranet to look through Bak's photographs again. In one of them, a faint blue moon hung between two tall buildings. In another, the afternoon sun streamed into the boy's study, illuminating the dust fluttering in the air and the sheets of paper, loose change, paintbrushes, dried paint, books, and a few incomplete sketches strewn over the desk. The last photograph showed a boy's pale, empty gaze. A weight pressed down on my eyelids, and soon I fell asleep in front of my laptop and into a dream.

"Never look into someone's eyes. It's dangerous. You don't know what the consequences will be," Aunt Myrtle said. Here, she had yet to conjoin with somebody. Every Sunday, she would come at sunset to our apartment to visit me and my mother, and before dinner was ready, she would sit me on her lap and lean close to my ear to whisper things I didn't understand. Many years later, digging through old magazines at the university library, I would sometimes come across her photoshoots—Aunt Myrtle in a form-fitting black turtleneck dress, glancing at the camera at an angle. Remnants of what she'd said to me drifted through my mind like the sporadic murmurs of a distant wind.

When I woke up, I realized that it hadn't been a dream

at all, but something that had actually taken place in the past. In the days to follow, like reflections on the pupil of an eye, the afterimage of the photographs infiltrated my mind in the most unexpected moments. They appeared as I watched a train go past, as I waited for water to boil, and as I looked up a word in the dictionary. At night, I lay in bed but couldn't close my eyes. I also lost my appetite, as if I'd been struck by some unknown disease.

In the early hours of my first sleepless night, May placed a warm glass of water on my bedside table and asked, "What's wrong?"

"Those photos, they're like knives. My life was per-fectly fine before they slashed everything to tatters," I told her.

She only smiled. "Nothing is that powerful." Then she slipped back into her bed. It felt like she wasn't taking me seriously, but a long time later, I understood that maybe she just lacked the courage to face things as they were.

⌒

I was at the end of the corridor, standing outside the door of Professor Foot's office to read the news clipping he'd taped on the square glass window. It was an article about

the Guantánamo Bay camp in Cuba, which detained prisoners without trial. The detainees were subject to so many
types of torture, they would rather kill themselves in the
most appalling ways. Even though the American guards
confiscated every conceivable tool they had and bound
their hands and legs, the prisoners still found ways to end
their lives, biting off their tongues or hanging themselves
with blankets.

Many called for the closure of the prison, but a Cuban
artist was proposing to turn it into a museum instead.
All the military personnel and detainees would remain
and everything would be kept the way it was, including
the various kinds of torture. The only difference was that
the institution would be open to the public, and visitors
could tour the building. "Not to showcase violence,
because violence doesn't actually exist here—the guards
are only exercising their duties, and the detainees,
guilty or innocent, have already been marked as evil.
Visitors can use this place as a release for the obligatory
compassion they ought to have, like sewage in need of a
drain. There is only one goal for the museum: to show
how abusers perpetuate abuse, how the abused remain
subject to abuse, and how bystanders carry on being
passive spectators. It'll be like an immersive theater,

where pain is no longer felt." This was how the artist explained his concept.

I walked into the office, and Professor Foot stopped what he was doing and trained his eyes on me. I stared right back at him. Ever since we touched each other's bodies, we'd stopped avoiding each other's eyes—not because we'd gained an understanding of each other, but because we had less of that inexplicable fear between people. I got straight to the point. "Will Bak come visit our class again?"

"The next guest lecturer is a quadriplegic, whose wheelchair has become part of his body. For the first ten years after his car accident, he laid in bed completely immobile. He was clearly conscious, but was diagnosed as a vegetable, unable to communicate with the outside world," Professor Foot said with an ambiguous grin that I wasn't able to decipher.

"I won't be able to attend the next two classes."

"Why?"

"I need to conduct another experiment," I said. "For my paper, my fieldwork."

"What kind of experiment?" he asked, puzzled.

"I'm going to make Bak one of my research subjects; I'll try and be in his world." I couldn't help but hesitate, then I added, "Maybe go along with him while he does his photography work."

⌣

Bak's voice on the phone sounded like a tumble of boulders being pushed down a cliff, plunging into the depths of the sea one after the other. After I briefly explained my thesis and methodology, he warned me, "I never know where I'll end up taking my photos. It takes a lot of effort to find the right place, and I don't mean a walk in the park or some nice trip."

We met at a train station by the foot of a hill when it was high noon, the sun blazing overhead. I watched Bak get out of a car, his clothes pale as the sky in the distance. We nodded in greeting, then he turned and started walking. We didn't exchange a single word, pretending we weren't right next to each other, and the only sound we could hear was our rustling steps on the grass.

We climbed up a slope, then some stone steps onto a small, flat path, followed by yet another slope. Once we made a turn, we came to a place where the scenery looked both familiar and completely new. During the walk, I saw so many different species of trees and plants, but I couldn't identify any of them. Occasionally, a nameless bird soared above us, casting a small patch of shade on the ground like a momentary cloud. Bak's shadow lengthened as the sun traveled across the sky; at first, his shadow was far in front of me, then, slowly but surely, it flowed in my direction like water. Soon I was stepping on his shadow, and my shadow merged with his until I could no longer make out its distinct shape. That afternoon, the long hike reminded me of my lack of exercise, heart pounding and breathing erratic, and I couldn't help but think of all the physical degeneration and complications that could arise from conjoinment. But at that moment, to my surprise, I thought maybe those conditions weren't so scary after all.

We kept going until we reached a lookout on top of a hill. He stood in front of a wooden bench and pointed at a dam in the distance. "Over there."

I wasn't sure if he really wanted me to see something, or if it was one of those situations where someone had to speak to prevent the other from going astray. I sat on the grass, straining my eyes at the scenery, but all I could see was the reservoir, the undulating hills on the far side, and the roads, cars, wild dogs, and pavilions concealed among the myriad shades of green, a disordered mélange like every hour and every day that had gone by.

"Do you see it?" he asked after a while.

I shook my head. "Not really, it all looks the same." I stood next to him, noticing that the space between us was about the same as the distance between his head and his heart.

"Then what did you come to see?" he asked, perplexed. It could be impatience or disbelief in his voice, I couldn't say for certain.

"The things you see." I chose my words carefully. "Not through the lens of your camera, but your eyes." Once I spoke, silence fell around us, except for the crows, now calling out in vain.

"Well, then…" he paused before continuing, "climb up. Use me as a piece of rope, a flight of stairs, a water pipe." He put down his backpack and camera.

I took a breath, deciding that he was a ladder, removed my shoes, and placed my feet on his thighs. I climbed up his waist and arms, and he steadied me until I was hanging securely from his body, my head level with his.

"Do you see it now?" he asked.

Beyond the rolls of hills, the fields of grass, the reservoir, and the people was a fathomless sky, vast beyond words, enveloping everything else in sight. There were no clouds, only an enigmatic blue, and the wind, surreptitiously pulling those who were unaware into that arresting shade.

"What a strange blue," I uttered, then I promptly shut my mouth, suppressing an emotion within me that was quickly brewing into something dangerous.

⌣

After that, the turns of the hands of the clock lost their meaning and I could no longer track them to start or finish anything, and my daily routine started to disintegrate. There was a hole in the life that had cradled me like a net, the tear growing so large I was about to fall through.

I was absent for all my classes and stopped working on my dissertation. Even when I closed my eyes, I couldn't rest.

"I'm not the same person I was before," I told everyone else. For several months, I had been unable to fall asleep easily. During that time, people who longed for company after class or were struggling with their thesis would wander from the academic building at the top of the hill to the room May and I shared. They would stand briefly by my bed, holding my hand and peering at my forehead without a sound. "It's like some switch has been activated, and now I'm gradually losing control of my body," I said to anyone who visited. At first they comforted me with soft voices, but after a while, they just turned away and pretended not to hear me. When sunset was near and they left to return to their own rooms, only May stayed, lighting cigarettes and positioning her body to listen, even though there wasn't much I could say.

"Tell me more about this tear," May coaxed after she exhaled a smoke ring.

"I don't know if it could really be called a tear," I said, leaning against the wall. Maybe I hadn't actually lost anything. That blue sky above those ridges of hills had birthed so many fantasies that were coming alive in my head at an irrepressible speed. For no reason at all, I believed this had been bound to happen—if not in the past, then certainly in the future.

"What fantasies?" she asked.

I told her about moments in the wilderness, and the streetlights, building hallways, grocery stores. "Just ordinary things, only there's this undetectable crack in them… Could be the smallest shift in light or angle or color, differences our eyes can't make out but show a whole new world."

"That just means you've had enough of the reality you see in front of you," May said dispassionately.

"No." I quickly defended myself, but didn't know what I could say to make her understand. I felt like I'd lost not only my ability to sleep, but also the language to communicate with others. "My world has been invaded, crushed, by another world. Any structure or direction that I had has crumbled to pieces."

May took another drag, and then we stopped speaking, as if doing so would only bring us to the wall of a dead-end street.

One afternoon, May was out. No one was in the room but me. A sudden, irresistible impulse made me shoot out of bed. I threw on some clothes without looking at them and ran to the academic building—to Professor Foot's office.

I didn't look at the window, didn't even knock on the door, just walked straight in toward his desk. He lifted his head, eyes betraying no element of surprise. Before I could open my mouth, he said, "You're skipping too many classes."

"I'm also going nowhere with my thesis," I said.

"Why are you here then?"

"My fieldwork. I've fallen into the trap researchers face in their studies."

He raised an eyebrow. "You do realize that every trap is unique, that they're not all the same?"

"But what does that matter?" I told him I was losing my objectivity as a researcher, and how frightening it was: I was starting to doubt the basis of my dissertation.

"Maybe people who acquiesce to the conjoinment policy aren't forced to compromise, but are acting on an inscrutable desire within their bodies. Maybe there just hasn't been a stronger force discouraging this pursuit, which is admitting that they are indeed incomplete and imperfect on their own, that their bodies must be severed, penetrated, joined with another person's to be at ease, however false and short-lived that may be. Once the Conjoinment Act was put in place, they could comply with the legislation, as was their true inner wish, while transferring their feelings of denial and resistance onto the law itself. With that, people get to find a balance between body and mind."

The words that came out of my mouth shocked and embarrassed me, but Professor Foot was unperturbed. "Then just change the argument of your thesis. This always happens with fieldwork anyway. There's no use standing your ground on meaningless principles."

"But this isn't what I should believe," I retorted. I told

him, if my research was to proceed toward this conclusion, it would crumble me into a pile of shapeless matter, never to be pieced back together again.

"Fine, then let's reassemble your argument," he quipped, as if this was nothing but a joke to him. "It's also fine if you can't finish your thesis—in the end, most people don't."

"How is that okay?" I cried, hearing the shrill tremor in my voice, my body shaking with the outburst. "Aren't you supposed to guide me, to help me finish my paper?"

Professor Foot started laughing, laughing until he couldn't stop, his eyes brimming with tears. He wheezed and said, "Do you know what a dissertation supervisor is supposed to do? We're here so students can vent all their negative emotions. It's like I'm no different than that conjoinment law. How did this even happen?"

I didn't reply. Suddenly, I glimpsed myself in the window, which meant that night was already closing in. In the reflection, I saw my messy, knotted hair and wrinkled sweatshirt, so out of place with the photocopier, teacups, and neatly shelved books in the room. Utterly ashamed, I burst from the professor's office without saying goodbye and ran outside.

There was no one in the parking lot of the academic

building or on the path leading away from it, or outside the restaurant at the far end. Not even the stray cats that usually lingered in the flower beds were there. I slowed my steps.

In the dead of the sunset, I was completely alone. I felt an unexpected tranquility, a strange surge of glee.

⌒

I couldn't figure out if the place where I was to meet Bak was on the rooftop of the building or elsewhere.

The building had a pink facade. I raised my head, trying to discern the top, but the piercing sunlight made it hard to keep my eyes open. The minute hand of my watch was about to hit the mark of our appointed time, so I hurried into the lobby. Not wanting to wait, I skipped the elevator and pushed open the door next to the management office, which led to the back side of a flight of stairs. It was a surface made of multiple slopes rising steeply toward each other and wasn't meant for walking at all, nor was it well maintained or regularly cleaned. Most of the time, the back was wet and perilous, but it was still the quickest route to many destinations, which was why people used it all day long.

As I strode from slope to slope, a young Indian woman wearing a saree, scarlet and embroidered with gold, fell through the broken railing of the upper level of the building. She plunged headfirst, smashing her skull. Her mother's high-pitched wail was like the cry of some wounded animal. All the pedestrians who had been in a rush halted in their tracks, as if they had just seen an enactment of their own unknowable future.

I froze on the steps, unable to lift my feet. All of a sudden, I wasn't sure which way was the right direction, only that no matter if I went up or down, I must first pass through death, someone else's or my own.

When I woke, my phone had already been ringing for a long time.

"I'll meet you at the mirror place," Bak suggested on the other end of the line.

"Why are we going there?" I asked.

"To see the photos. The ones we took on the hill."

In anticipation of the mirrors that were installed everywhere—in the washroom, at the main entrance, on the ceiling, on the tabletops and chairs, I changed into a cropped leather jacket and mini skirt, tied my hair up, and put on some light pink blush and lip gloss. Only when I felt like my body was a shell that didn't belong to me did I leave the room May and I shared.

Bak was seated on a couch next to a mirror, so when I walked toward him, it looked like there were two identical people sitting there, making me almost bump into the mirror.

"Where are the photos?" I sat down across from him.

"Don't know." He spread out his hands. "But we can still look through them together while the memory of what we saw is still fresh in our minds."

I peered over the top of his head, my eyes falling on the pillar at the center of the restaurant, the hanging lights, the seats around us, the backs of the servers, and finally on the mirror beside us. In that strange moment, I discovered that the restaurant in the mirror didn't look exactly the same as the room I was in. They were two distinct spaces, only I couldn't pinpoint their differences or even figure out which was the reflection, the copy. I spotted two people in the mirror; their features resembled me and Bak, and I couldn't help but wonder what kind of people they were and why they were there, their relationship, and, when they were to leave, what kind of future they each held. I hadn't expected Bak to also turn his head and stare into the mirror at a similar angle, as though he were also searching for something—a hunched angler looking out for traces of fish. When it occurred to me to stop him, it was already too late.

The bright morning sun dappled the tips of our hair and our arms. I looked back and forth between us: my bony palms and his thick palms; my pale neck, his tanned neck; his overly long legs, my scrawny legs; his brown clothes, my blindingly black outfit. Then I saw what he saw.

"It's all right," I said.

If our bodies are intrinsic to who we are, and who we are determines our distance from people, then our reflections in the mirror had already predicted the different directions we would soon embark upon.

Time, then, was meaningless, no matter if we spent two days, two years, or twenty years together. Beneath the sun, the silhouette he cast on the ground was very thin, very narrow—a boat sailing into a secret shore of my mind. Later, the sun never disappeared from there, and always brought with it an intense shadow.

Before we said goodbye, I took him to a park next to the mirror place. The elderly people had already finished their morning exercises and gone home, and the children had not yet finished school, so the park was mostly empty.

"Let me tell you a story," I said as we walked under an oleander tree.

"Who is this story about?" he asked.

"It hasn't happened yet, but it exists in every universe. Still, will you listen?"

He didn't say anything, so I started from the very beginning. The story was about a person who never brought an umbrella when going out, someone who truly believed that, although humans live on land, they all start their lives immersed in their mothers' amniotic fluid. Not only should they not be afraid of water, they should seize every chance there is to swim.

⌒

This is an instinct that will soon be forgotten. These were the only words that came to their mind when they looked out the window, watching rain pour like a cascade of beads as the sky belted out a furious rumble. The weather service had issued warnings for heavy rain and landslides that morning. Naturally, they hadn't packed an umbrella in their briefcase for the commute to work.

You'll get drenched in this weather anyway. Better to just let water seep into your body, they thought.

When they reached the lobby of their building, it was already filled with a crowd of people hunching over, rolling up their sleeves and pants in preparation for a journey into the water. A security guard came up and said, "The flood is really serious." He placed a hand by his waist to show the water level. Heeding the security guard's advice, the person removed their shoes and watch.

They followed the other residents from the building, whom they had never met before, and one by one, people leaped into the water beyond the fence of the premises, pushing their arms and legs to paddle. This reminded the person of the swimming competitions they had been in as a kid, and they marveled at the wondrousness of the situation. At first, people were laughing and squealing in delight at getting to soak in the cool rainwater on a hot summer day, but after a while, there was nothing but the sound of labored breathing. None of the swimmers could ignore all the trash and dead insects floating around, or the microbes that might be in the water. They had no choice but to be vigilant every time they dipped their heads, and that made it impossible to enjoy the swim.

The person also realized that the submerged road was steeper and more rugged than they remembered. Soon their feet could no longer touch the ground, and the farther they swam, the more they flailed to stay afloat. At first, there were many residents swimming in much the same way, but every time the person pushed their head above water, they saw fewer and fewer people around them. They couldn't tell if it was because the others had given up and returned to where they came from, or if everyone had arrived at their destinations. Then the person noticed a strange reaction on their hands and arms: they were turning white, wrinkled and swollen, scaly lumps rising across their skin as it became slimy to the touch, like some putrid kind of fish. Their head grew heavy all of a sudden. Even though the streets had been decimated by the flood, they could still make out a vermillion rooftop nearby on the left. The person remembered who lived in that house, someone they felt close to but rarely contacted. So they swam in that direction, thinking they could pay a visit and step foot into their place with the excuse of feeling unwell—and with that thought in mind, the irritation from the scales on their skin seemed to subside.

⌣

"Do you think that person is a man or a woman?" I asked him.

"Gender isn't important," he answered. Then I asked him what their relationship to the person in the house might be.

"Friends, neighbors, teacher and student…" He looked deep in thought, and then he said, "Or maybe it's a relationship so undefinable, they don't know how to be with each other."

I was sure he was listening, so I continued.

⌣

The woman saw a man standing outside her door, drenched and covered in scales. He pointed at his mouth, but no sound came out. She thought he resembled the tropical fish she had as a pet when she was a child. When the fish died, she was watching it through the glass, unable to save its life as it sank to the bed of artificial rocks and stopped moving. She let the man into her house, helped him take off his suit jacket, and loosened the tie that had been tight around his neck. Since she couldn't get him to say anything, she ran a full tub of warm water for him, laid him inside, and massaged the swollen lumps on his body. He looked at her, unable to speak, and she could see herself reflected in his eyes. The color of his irises reminded her of someone, but she couldn't remember who no matter how hard she tried. Ever since the city's temperature had started rising and the air became thick with exhaust that never dissipated, her memory had begun deteriorating. She sighed, lamenting her forgetful self, and headed to her living room, tidying the space and wiping the couch in case he needed to stay the night. She didn't dare treat him any less courteously, worrying that he might be someone incredibly important to her, only that she had forgotten.

She returned to the bathroom, humming a tune now that all the cleaning was done, only to find most of the water in the tub gone, and his face and body overgrown with glossy gray scales. She reached out to touch him, and he was cold and hard. She put a finger under his nose— he was no longer breathing. A fishy odor permeated her home. At a loss for what to do, she kneeled by the bathtub in distress until her legs grew numb. She went and rummaged through the briefcase he'd left behind, but couldn't find anything that might help identify him. Exhausted, she lay on the floor and eventually fell asleep. For several days, she slept and woke, woke and slept again, not wanting to get up at all, until sunlight beamed through the window and fell on her face, the warmth making her stir. She sat up, still in a daze, drawing her knees to her chest, before she finally stood and headed into the bathroom again. She dragged his body to the yard outside her small house, found a stool, and sat, watching over him.

Her neighbor, walking past with a friend, noticed what she was doing and came to praise her. "What a big fish you've caught! It must be freshwater…no, from the sea."

The woman nodded, unsure of how to respond.

Her neighbor's friend said, "Chop it up and it'll feed you for days. Or, you could cure and sun-dry the meat to preserve it for longer." Having offered their opinions, the pair walked away, leaving the woman with her dashed hopes—she had wished that exposure to some ultraviolet light would disinfect and cure him, and turn him back to who he had been.

When the sun was obscured once more by polluted clouds, she dragged him back into the house like she was collecting laundry from a clothesline. She spread a layer of salt over him and waited for the sun to rise the next day before moving him to the yard again. A plan began to formulate in her head—she would sun-dry his body and order a custom-made wooden box, and then she would wrap him in newspaper and store him inside. She knew she could keep his body for a long time once it was cured. She would even put the box under her bed so she could fall asleep inhaling his salty fragrance. And then, when she was about to face her own death, she would prepare a pot of rice and a bottle of liquor, take him out of the box after years of curing, and eat him with rice. Once she'd absorbed all the nutrients he had to give, she would die, and her funeral would be a service for two people. It was a conscientious arrangement. To prevent herself from forgetting, she wrote it down in a notebook, which she took out to reread from time to time.

⌣

"It's not such a tragic tale, is it?" I asked him.

He shook his head and got to his feet, raising his hand like he was going to pick a flower from the oleander tree. I stood on a wooden chair and took a hemp rope from my bag. I wrapped it tightly around him from the top, from his forehead over his cheeks, neck, shoulders, chest, torso, hips, legs, all the way to the soles of his feet, encircling him in ring after ring. He didn't resist, keeping his body ramrod straight like a mummy, and so I was grateful for his cooperation. Once I was done, I cut the rope at the end with a pair of scissors and freed him. He left the park from the east entrance, I from the north gate.

We didn't intend on seeing each other ever again.

As for the length of rope I had used to measure Bak's body, I put it on my bed at first, wondering what to do with it. I could use it to scale a hill or a cliff, or wrap it around my neck and choke myself. I ended up bringing the rope with me in my bag. Every time I went out, whenever there was a free moment, I felt compelled to wrap the rope around trees, light poles, telephone booths, and road signs, but nothing ever matched its length. At that, I always let out a sigh of relief, as though I were going through a series of trials. In the end, I stored the rope in a corner of my closet. It coiled around itself like a hibernating snake, though I was certain it would never wake.

All the while, my insomnia worsened, and I grew to understand that in certain states of existence, to live was really just another form of death.

Outline, Part II

II. Hidden Desires

How does fear take root and blossom in a person's heart? In the book *The Power Within*, Stephen Johnson writes about an experiment on self-actualization, in which he concludes (albeit arbitrarily) that life is a play entirely of one's own staging. Whenever people complain about their misfortunes, rarely do they know that these inscrutable twists of fate actually spawn from the anxieties and fears hidden in their subconscious. These emotions evolve into desires so exceptionally strong, they end up inciting terrible spectacles in real life.

For their decade-long experiment, Johnson and his research team sent over 3,000 letters inviting people from different social backgrounds and professions to participate. In the letter, Johnson claimed, *Subjects are only required to visit the research center once a month*

*and discuss their psychological state. They also con-
sent to letting our agents follow and observe them in
their everyday lives. Other than that, they can go about
their days as usual.* Five hundred people wrote back
to express their interest. Most were incentivized by the
free counseling, while a small portion signed up just to
stop the pestering researchers who kept visiting their
workplaces to recruit them.

Later, Johnson divided the subjects into twenty-five
groups. Each group was locked in a dark room with the
lights off and windows covered, and each subject was
blindfolded with a strip of black cloth before entering the
room. A researcher instructed them to move, holding
onto the subject's arm as they felt their way forward,
encouraging them and saying, "There's a fire in front of
you, but with enough faith, you can walk through it un-
harmed." Some of the subjects refused to keep going,
and some shook with so much terror, they tumbled onto
the floor in agony before reaching the place where the
fire was supposed to be. Others were convinced they
had already been severely burned and filled the room
with anguished howls and curses. When a subject could
no longer bear the test and ripped off the blindfold, they
would find that the room was completely empty except

for a round pillar at the center and the stench of roast meat wafting in the air.

The purpose of Johnson's experiment was not to demonstrate that people are driven by fear, but how our visceral desires tend to reveal themselves in twisted and insidious ways. The subjects who agreed to being tracked and observed for ten years eventually formed the dataset for Johnson's assertions, and the monthly consultations were his primary method to analyze the subjects' behaviors.

During the research period, feminist campaigner X assisted countless sex workers evicted by the police and gangs, domestic helpers exploited by their agents and employers, and women abused by their husbands. In that time, X had also gone through three divorces from marriages in which she experienced violence. Johnson interprets X this way: "Strictly speaking, she is not a victim in the usual sense, but so zealous about women's liberation that she believes she must make some form of sacrifice to fully empathize with the women she campaigns for, hence her attraction to men with a history of violence."

O was the CEO of a public company selling leather apparel when he was younger, and lived in a mansion on a hill. After the economic crisis, he admitted himself into a charity shelter and worked part-time as a security guard. In Johnson's opinion, this had nothing to do with financial ruin, but O's warped concept of money as a person who grew up in a resettlement estate.

"He saw wealth like the wind, something that would eventually escape him, and thought that an incessant pursuit of financial gain was foolish." Johnson describes O to be so high-strung, he would only feel relief the day his money evaporated from his bank account, even though he would look miserable and depressed on the outside. These cases, according to Johnson's explanation, are instances of intrinsic desire manifesting as distorted expressions of anxiety. As dreams that do not conform to society's common values get realized, their fulfillment also brings to their achievers an accompanying sense of guilt.

"An empty heart will always find a way to fill itself," he writes, believing that O and X had gotten what they wanted, but not without a price.

For all these years, have people's perceptions of conjoinment also been fear and desire like Johnson describes—psychological complexes that are much the same, with the same origin? How has this affected the trajectory of society's position on conjoined people?

In the nineteenth century, conjoined people were seen as monsters, and so circuses and expos were the few places where they could make a living, even though they were excruciatingly exploited. This was hardly a secret for the crowds who marveled as conjoined people sang, played the saxophone, and danced on stage, as if they were born jolly and with these talents. The audience must have imagined beneath the extravagant costumes the bodies that had two chests, hips, and even genitalia. They knew it was common for conjoined people to be sold by their guardians, capitalized for money, trafficked, overworked, and sexually assaulted, and that these things happened with the tacit approval of the public, as if they were the necessary prerequisites to tame a beast. In these circuses and expos, conjoined people were no different from lions jumping through hoops of fire or bears on unicycles. Rather than for the wonderful performances, every scream or cheer the audience gave out was for how they finally got to be close to these fearful freaks, which came to them as domesticated clowns or humble servants for their entertainment, making them feel less insignificant in the face of this wide world.

Since the twentieth century, as separation surgery became more common and people had other sources of pleasure, conjoined people gradually disappeared from this function and became a media hot topic (the advancement of human rights also made it impossible for the audience to enjoy the performances). Surgical separation became the subject of numerous headlines and oftentimes moral debate—like the death of Iranian twin sisters Ladan and Laleh Bijani from a failed operation, and Taiwanese brothers Chang Chung-jen and Chang Chung-i, whose surgery was successful, but also enabled them to commit a financial scam.

The Brian Whitman case is generally thought of as a watershed moment, bringing to an end the notion of a clear demarcation between conjoined/individual and normal/deviant.[1] If Martin Stewart's theory, comparing consciousness to a mirror in the heart, is taken to be true, then an embryo splitting only partially and birthing conjoined infants is a material reflection of our deepest unconscious desire as people—a simultaneous coveting and fear of interdependence with another human body. Thus, on a conscious level, there is no precise line to be drawn between the conjoined and the individual, or between normal and deviant. Even if Brian

Whitman had not fought in court for the right to attach his deceased wife's arm to his body, conjoinment would still have become an unavoidable phenomenon via some other event, or in some other form, as a manifestation of our minds.

---

[1] A court case over a body between relatives in the 1980s, also known as the landmark case that indirectly created a precedent for the Conjoinment Act. Two weeks after his wife died jumping off a building, Brian Whitman, a bank teller, submitted an application to the court to amputate her left arm so that he could connect it to his left shoulder. Although many doctors warned him there was little chance of the arm functioning even if the postmortem blood vessels were successfully connected, Whitman insisted on the procedure. He believed that a part of his wife's soul remained in her deceased body, and that it didn't matter to anyone but him. In the ten years they lived together, they had built their lives to become inextricable. He was used to her holding his right hand when watching movies and having her on his left as he ate. She helped him blow dry his hair when he washed it late at night, and he held her left hand in his right whenever they went out. When

they hugged, her right arm rested just above his tailbone, and so on and so forth. Whitman listed a hundred habits, odors, ways of speaking, and routines he had shared with his wife to prove that there were many intimate parts of his wife's body that belonged to him. "I won't be able to live if you separate us," he said. "While immeasurable and intangible, the impact this will have on me is of greater consequence than losing a vital organ." He challenged the rigidity of the law, which he said reduced differences between people but exacerbated inequality. His claims were vehemently refuted by the wife's family, who fought to keep their daughter's body intact. In the end, the court ruled in Whitman's favor. For the duration of the trial, the wife's body was stored in a custom-made mortuary freezer.

Requiem

I no longer had any hope of returning to normal sleep. My surroundings, the faces and voices of the people I knew, my thesis, and my days and nights had all fallen into a disunity of fragments, losing some crucial connection. I thought this would eventually become a new kind of life, but May didn't agree with me at all.

"Losing the ability to fall asleep is a sign that your body's rhythm has been disrupted." May was reading from a magazine article by a sleep therapist. "Nevertheless, practice can restore order." She'd lit some supposedly calming incense in a corner of our room and was playing records of piano études at a soothing volume all day long. "For insomniacs, sound is just as important as temperature," she continued, draping a comforter over me before walking back to her computer to resume her work. I started to cry, feeling that my strength was slipping away with my tears to someplace I couldn't name. I didn't know why May was doing all of this; it wasn't like we were living in the same body, so my predicament had no real bearing on her whatsoever. Eventually, it occurred to me that since we lived in the same room, the misery of my insomnia might be transmitted to her side of the space through the particles in the air. And so, to stop my insomnia from disrupting May's life as much as possible, I shut my eyes and lay flat on the bed every night when the clock struck twelve, keeping my breathing even and trying not to toss and turn until morning came. After a week, I started to wonder if this was another kind of sleep, though I remained wide awake without a single lapse in consciousness.

And then one morning, May came over to my bed with joy lighting up her face. She clasped my hand and said, "You fell asleep, did you know? You've been sleeping every night." I looked at her flushed cheeks and smile, and knew that she believed the piano music and incense were healing me.

"We can now start the next phase of your treatment." She'd booked an appointment for me with the sleep therapist who wrote the article. His clinic was in a building next to a wet market that was about to be demolished. The market floor was slippery with grime and littered with meat and vegetable scraps. Men moving goods on trolleys hurtled and hollered around us, but since I was with May, I might as well have been walking in an open field. She held my hand the entire way, her palm soft and supple, like she was cradling my entire person. Fortune tellers have said that women with palms like that are destined to become the wives of wealthy men.

It was a Wednesday morning. May and I stepped into an elevator. The elevator took us to a door, which opened, and then we walked until we reached the end of a corridor, where another door stood. May signaled for me to go into that room by myself.

"I'm headed off to class. I'll see you later tonight." She gave me a little wave.

Standing inside, I watched May's figure recede, feeling like those who suffer from sleep disorders are simply people who have fallen through the cracks—others may turn or walk around the gap with ease, while we've stumbled right into it, unable to extract ourselves.

The room was furnished with a white single bed and chair. I stayed close to the walls, deliberating over where to sit before finally choosing the chair. It wasn't a comfortable chair, but sitting on it, I could look at a painting hanging from the ceiling. The painting looked like a cloudless night sky gleaming with iridescence. At first I thought the vibrant colors were drawn with pigments, but then I saw that they were flies, butterflies, bees, and other insects stuck on the paper at their moment of death. As I stared at their wings, incoherent fragments—the backs of people and their hair, spray from a puddle driven over by a car, a sinister-looking cloud, railings, windblown trash—flitted wildly before my vision until everything became a blur.

I wasn't aware that the sound of breathing had infiltrated the room and my ears. By the time I registered the inhales and exhales punctuating the fragments I was seeing and turned my head, a stout man was already sitting on the bed, holding a silver timer in his hand.

"Five minutes and forty-six seconds." He stopped the timer. "Normally, it takes around three minutes for people with sleep disorders to react to a shift in the room's atmosphere. Those who need five minutes or longer have moderately severe disorders."

"Is that so?" I replied, fixing my gaze on the fading paint on the wall. Suddenly I felt just how cramped the room was, and reminded myself of the fact that he was someone who cured insomnia.

"You don't have to do anything today," he said in a reassuring tone. "We'll only start doing exercises next week." I had no way of letting him know that I didn't need any reassurance.

"First, I'm going to walk you through the specifics of your treatment. This is where you'll practice sleeping. Familiarize yourself with the room; you'll only sleep soundly if you do," he said, still sitting on the white bed as though he'd just woken up. The sight of him made me suddenly afraid of losing the freedom to stay awake, though I couldn't say why.

"Next to this room is another room, which has yet another room right next to it. All of our rooms here are arranged by how deeply you sleep. Every time we move over one room, it means that your condition has improved." He knocked on the wall and continued. "Most of the patients next door are clerks or office workers taking some respite from their work. Once they've grasped a method of rest, they can get all the energy they need for the day with just a little bit of sleep." He looked at me and lifted the corners of his mouth, a smile meant to put me at ease. "There's really not much to worry about. Most people don't get enough sleep anyway, and even if they do, the quality of their sleep is far from ideal."

I didn't make a sound, only diverted my eyes to the far side of the room. As a patient suffering from a sleep disorder, I knew I had the right to keep my face blank.

You don't believe me? We're all born with the ability

to sleep effectively; we just gradually forget as we grow older," he said. "Everyone sleeps for ten whole months in the womb, saving up enough energy to last a lifetime before leaving their mother's body. We fall back asleep when our lives end and we can no longer relieve our fatigue. Most people call it death without understanding that it's really just much-needed slumber."

I turned my head to the side to stare out the window, but there was nothing to see other than an excavated construction site, where a few helmeted workers wandered aimlessly.

"A fetus's sleep in their mother's body has a critical impact on the rest of their life, but few people pay attention to how crucial sleep is, much less the significance it holds." He proceeded to illustrate his point with his own experiences. I looked at the four walls of the room, feeling his voice suffuse every crack and corner, and wondered if his incessant talking was to adapt me to the cadence of his speech.

He starting telling me about his mother, a performer. Ever since she was a teenager, his mother had aspired to become a pianist in an orchestra, playing for an opera or in a concert hall, but many years passed and she was still performing in shopping malls, bars, and fancy restaurants.

"She held onto that dream even though it didn't come true. By keeping a dream that has no bearing on reality, you keep yourself in a state of youth. She must have understood this well." Then he talked about the changes in her body when she was pregnant with him. "It was a time of abundance. She was lonelier than ever before, but fulfilled." He stopped briefly, an almost imperceptible pause, before he continued to speak. "The same could be said for me, maybe, I'm not sure; it's been years and I'm still figuring it out."

Once his mother's weight and figure became visibly different, he said, she locked herself inside her small home and rarely went out except for groceries and other essential errands. While her belly grew bigger and her body swelled, her mind was inundated by all the accidents that might happen and she became extra sensitive and cautious about everything, as if the world beyond the small space she lived in was nothing but danger. "If given the chance, she would've turned completely transparent for a while so that she could disappear until the baby was born and life went back to normal."

Her changed body made it impossible for her to avoid physical contact with other people. Large and sluggish, she blocked the way of hustling pedestrians at subway entrances, forcing them to slow down until they shot impatient looks at her. She was convinced that the world consisted of only her and the child in her belly, especially when her morning sickness was so severe that she wasn't able to eat or go about her day. She consulted her obstetrician, but the advice she received was completely useless, and so she communicated with her growing fetus using her own methods to soothe its inexplicable restlessness. To calm her frequent urge to vomit, the aggressive tossing and turning of her child, and the hormonal disruptions to her mood, she recited Bach's music in her head and played the opuses over and over using her round belly as a keyboard until her discomfort receded like the tide. Sometimes, her mind was ambushed by a series of nightmarish thoughts: her face ripped to shreds by a cat; the bloated, purplish flesh of a drowned woman; her belly sliced open while she was asleep, her unborn baby gone. But once she pressed her fingers to her abdomen and breathed to the rhythm of the music, she felt she could see the light again.

She firmly believed that only she and her child could understand each other, so when her obstetrician warned her she was overdue and that it was dangerous for her to not have shown signs of labor, she rejected the recommendation to get a Cesarean and only pressed her lips into a thin line without arguing. In her heart, she knew her baby only needed to sleep for a little longer; maybe it was just timid and hadn't amassed enough courage to begin its long life. She didn't push, didn't encourage, only lay in bed, hugging her belly to sleep, waiting patiently. She comforted her hesitant baby, saying, "It's fine even if you don't want to be born," and couldn't help but feel proud of herself for being such a competent mother.

"However," the sleep therapist said, "I've never known a woman better at making things difficult for others."

"Use your fingers; they're more effective than tears or drugs at getting rid of negative emotions." This was what the sleep therapist's mother had taught him since he was a toddler. As he grew up and stepped into puberty, her instructions became stricter and bordered on unreasonable. She urged him to meet lots of women, even laying down her own criteria: "Find someone who dances, with a flexible body." But at that time, other than piano, he was only interested in soccer, and everyone was a potential competitor, including every girl he knew, even if they looked as delicate as flowers that could wilt at any moment.

"Even if you don't date, you need to find someone to touch and talk to. Try to feel someone's skin and the bumps of their joints on your fingertips, then you'll understand what it means to play the piano," she said as a compromise, but even that seemed out of reach for him. From there, she began to place more specific restrictions, forbidding him from crying, raging, shouting, any behavior that expressed resentment. He was only allowed to explore the world through his fingertips, from walls to fish at the wet market to the hair of passengers sitting in front of him on a bus.

"Maybe she wasn't aware, was never aware, of the kinds of mortifying thoughts that plague an adolescent's mind." That year, he had a strong conviction that his mother wasn't trying to push him so that he would pass all his piano exams, but rather to become a piano he could play as he wished. This idea darkened his heart, and soon he avoided her in every corner of their home.

I watched the sleep therapist walk along the wall, approaching a cage in a zoo. His hands were soft and fair like calligraphy paper, brushing past each bar until he caressed an elephant's trunk, a lion's chin, the back of a koala, a vine of ivy, dolphins, and slumbering egrets. Suddenly it occurred to me how outlandish this looked in a clinic. I recalled the white floor and bedsheets, the lackluster colors, and then I opened my eyes.

"You've just experienced a short sleep." At some point,

the sleep therapist had stood up from his place on the bed, blocking my view of the window and casting his shadow over me.

"How long do I have to sleep before it's enough?" I asked.

"There's no need to rush. This is only your first time," he said, in the reserved and ambiguous tone therapists often use. "You must practice consistently, two hours a day at home. I've already told the friend who came with you what she should do."

He handed me two CDs. I glanced at the covers. Robert Schumann—the pianist who longed to be so virtuosic, he ruined one of his fingers and spent the rest of his days in a mental asylum.

⌣

When I returned to the dormitory, May was sitting in front of her desk. Ever since my sleep disorder disintegrated my old life, May was always in our room, as though she had become part of it. I never asked why she stayed in all the time for fear that her answer might be a taboo that, once exposed, would wake us from the haze of our moment, causing us to descend into the unknown. I handed her the

CDs; she took them and carefully read the short text on the covers.

"This therapist has no formal training. He's just good at making music with people's bodies," I told her.

"So?" She didn't look up as she spoke. "Most of the patients he's treated said that they can fall asleep again. Some sleep so deeply, they get to experience what it's like to be dead to the world."

"But how can we be sure these people aren't lying?" I asked. May fell silent, and I couldn't find the words to continue. All of a sudden, the air between us was so overgrown with thorns, every shift of our bodies seemed to lead to stabs of pain everywhere. May and I were not always talkative, and the silence we had was a harmony that allowed us to forget our own existence. At some point, this connection had abruptly severed, and everything surreptitiously veered onto a different course. I had no idea what caused this to happen, so I could only think of it as a side effect of my insomnia.

"Other than class, you've spent a long time hiding in this room. Have you figured out the problem with your thesis?" After much deliberation, I opened my mouth to stop our silence from spreading until it reached a fatal threshold. If it did, we would have no choice but to unearth all the issues that we'd left unspoken.

"The problems don't exist anymore, for my dissertation and graduation." She turned toward me, her eyes downcast as she smiled. "We'll only face the real challenges after we graduate and leave this dorm anyway." She took a deep breath, like she'd just made a difficult decision, then she slipped one of the CDs into the drive and let the music play.

I closed my eyes. At first the tune was unusually soft, like a pot of water that had yet to boil, reminding me of the background music in supermarkets and furniture stores. Suddenly, after a certain bar, it took a complete turn, becoming a rush of storm clouds, or a gallop of countless horses awakened from slumber, racing from afar to trample us.

"To a musician, getting admitted to a mental asylum must feel like an essential part of their career," I said as I lay on my bed.

"It's as important as their artistic accomplishments," May responded in a low voice.

"What a strange thing."

"It's not strange at all."

"Why?"

"Because they've gotten to a level beyond the reach of

ordinary people." She paused for a moment. "Madness."

The music coming from the computer became more persistent and intense; the stampede had arrived, and our thin door was about to splinter. I felt my body fall further from the mattress into a soft, dark place, my ears slowly filled to the brim with murmurs of wind, birdsong, and leaves flapping against each other. And then, once all of this was past, the disquiet that had been roiling beneath the tranquility surged—I was before an endless sky atop a hill, with flame-red light scorching through the clouds and the remains of an old moon fading in a corner of the atmosphere. The sun was intense that afternoon, and Bak was standing at the edge of the hill. I opened my eyes, to the gray of the ceiling above me.

◡

After scheduling my next appointment with the therapist, I told May that she didn't have to come with me to the clinic anymore. "I can get there myself. You're already so busy with class, and if you keep following me around, it'll look too much like one of us is a captive." May smiled weakly at that, a smile that made her look already trapped.

A nurse led me down the corridor, stopping at the

second to last room from the end, and gestured for me to go in. Like May, she also turned and left once I stepped inside.

The therapist was already standing before the window. He asked me how I was. "I bet your sleep has improved a little!" I couldn't cover up the truth; my condition hadn't gotten worse, but it hadn't gotten better either. But I also saw the eager look on his face and didn't have the heart to say what would only disappoint him, so I adopted a vague expression and shoved the CDs he'd given me as homework toward him.

"So? Have you listened to all of it?" He waved the CDs in his hand. I gave him a small nod.

"Let the music flow into your breathing and your bloodstream. This is how you can unfold all of yourself," he advised. I lowered my head and fiddled with my gown that smelled of detergent and antiseptic, running my fingers over the black staves, the tadpole-looking notes, and the bold keyboard design on the fabric. Inadvertently, the motion made me touch all the bony ridges of my upper body.

"Schumann's pieces have healing properties." He flapped the CDs in his hand again. "The best doctors are often deeply ill themselves." He was describing musicians who succumbed to insanity, but for some reason, I felt that he was really talking about himself. "Bach, on the other hand, is for people who already abide by the rules, who just need help not going off course."

After that, he gave me his commands. "Lie down on the bed. Relax and keep your body straight, and spread out your arms."

I positioned myself the way he directed and breathed to the rhythm of his breaths. I closed my eyes when he told me to and lost sight of the room's furnishing, decor, and the color of its walls, until I was left with a tumultuous darkness. His fingers, long and thin, were on my ribcage and thigh. Like a pianist about to start his performance, he softly added pressure with his fingertips.

"You are a piano, a black one," he said, his breath fanning my face. "In this part of the treatment, imagination is an indispensable element. Most cases of psychosis are caused by an overindulgent imagination, but the people subject to it aren't so much deranged as they are unusually attached to their dreams, so much so that when they wake, they continue to latch onto what they saw in their sleep, even if it's at odds with reality." His fingers started to dance across my skin in a rapid melody. I remembered the left part of my white gown was filled with a dense cluster of musical notes and rests, while the right part was a keyboard of rectangular keys. I almost burst out laughing at the sensation, but then I thought back to what he said: "You are a piano." At that moment, I understood he'd told me a truth I hadn't been aware of—all my problems originated from my misconception that I was a human being. So I kept my body ramrod straight, and no longer felt the urge to move.

"People with sleep disorders either have superb concentration, devoting so much of their minds to matters of the day that they aren't willing to take a break and get into the rhythm of sleep, or they lack the ability to pay attention, their brains constantly whirring over various things, so sleep is dull and lackluster by comparison. The first type of patient is more precarious because they're closer to madness, while the second type is more commonplace. Modern society is all about efficiency and the division of labor; it's a luxury to focus on one thing at a time. To bring adjustment to these minds, they need to be moderated until they neither overconcentrate nor get too distracted. Only then will they have the chance to fall into deep sleep." His voice was as light as the touch of his fingers, which no longer felt ticklish once I was attuned to the belief that I was just a piano. Underneath this gown was my body, and inside this physical shell was my soul, where I was hiding.

"When you first arrived, you were assigned to the room at the end, which means you belonged to the first type. However, with the right treatment, you'll still be able to return to regular sleep." These were words of encouragement, but I also heard the clear implication of a threat, which may have simply been a habit of his profession.

His fingertips started to feel like large droplets of rain falling on my abdomen. He began recounting moments from his past, his voice coalescing with the movements of his hands, his speech matching an inaudible tune, a piece I suspected was his own. It was a piece he could only play in his clinic, where he could find the ideal audience for his performance.

"My father disappeared after I was born. When I finished all the piano exams, my mother also stopped playing the piano." He believed these events were connected by a rhythm that suddenly made its presence heard. "It must have been there all along, only my mother kept it to herself."

Until one night, which was just like any other night except for its eerie silence, his mother abruptly got out of bed, sat on the couch, and dialed a series of numbers on the phone. After she repeated the numbers ten times, everything fell quiet again as if nothing had happened at all.

"If that was a piece of music, the only thing it served to reveal was the secret of her anxiety." As he lay in bed listening to the intermittent and monotone notes from the phone, he understood that his mother was showing symptoms of insomnia, as with most people in the city, and like a bottle tipped over, everything she'd kept secreted away and compartmentalized deep inside of her was gushing out all at once. She wouldn't have known that her every move was being observed, so everything she did that night must have been true. In the dark, with his hearing alone, he carefully evaluated her distress, and in no time, he was filled to the brim with all the things he was going to say to her. But when morning came, they faced each other in utter silence; the words that were to be profuse and emotional remained inside him without a proper release.

In truth, he also thought that he understood his father, that stranger who panicked when he witnessed his child being born. "It must have reminded him of his own arrival into the world," he said emphatically. He'd rehearsed the words he wanted to say to his mother in his heart over and over: "It's not you or me he hates, but himself, the people he chooses, the way he lives, and the world he's helped create." But every time the therapist felt the urge to open his mouth, the words he wanted to say to his mother were drowned out by the water reaching its boiling point, the news blaring from the television, or the renovation work in the neighboring apartment. He remembered his days living in their home to be long, a journey with no destination, and silent as a plant growing into a frenzy. The view from the windows was always a white haze, so he never saw any scenery.

In the months before his mother passed away, she became too weak to take care of herself, so he washed her, dressed her, fed her, and carried her to and from her wheelchair to the bed, but his most important task was to massage every agonizing part of her body with his fingertips. They would both purse their lips, as if they were attending a solemn event that forbade talking, and he knew in his heart that what was stopping them from communicating wasn't language, but the fingertips he had so meticulously trained all his life.

These memories slowly faded into the air, and the tapping of his fingers turned featherlight until his touch was no

longer there. I regained sensation in my limbs and muscles, and felt the texture of fabric on my skin.

"Can you guess the piece that I was playing?" he asked.

"*Träumerei?*"

He shook his head.

"*A Poet's Love?*"

"Your treatment hasn't yet yielded the desired results,"
he concluded. "Once you remember by touch the music
you've heard, and by sound the sensations on your skin,
we'll be able to say that your body that has been too tense
to sleep is starting to loosen up.

"In the end," he continued, "insomniacs are just people
who are too sealed within themselves."

⌣

Checkup. Yi Wan Road. 10 a.m.

Following the map May had drawn in my notebook
and her directions, I arrived at the hospital and saw that
the building was on the slope of a hill. Like the harbor,
which used to be wide, the hills around here had started
disappearing one by one. We weren't completely unaware
of the constant excavation and reclamation work, but
it was only when we saw straight, flat roads stretching

endlessly before us that the void left by all that was lost became truly palpable.

A newspaper article predicted that we would no longer see any mountain peaks, seas, or adult bodies that were whole in twenty years. We had grown accustomed to these horrifying speculations, the same way we read about faraway countries with long and foreign-sounding names wrecked by war, earthquakes, storms, and massacres. There would be a moment when we fell into wordless grief, but with the turn of a page, we would get inundated by job and real-estate listings and restaurant advertisements again. People weren't indifferent; it was just that, for those of us who lived here, the future always felt so surreal.

The hospital was rebuilt from a colonial-era Gothic church that was abandoned during the war. Compared to the homogeneous buildings in the area, it stood tall and aloof on the hill, like a species of bird that had already gone extinct. A public relations spokesperson from the hospital once claimed that it was pragmatic to make the facility a recognizable landmark—it was the only way to stop patients disoriented by their illnesses from wandering off.

Outside the reception was a long, narrow waiting area. Beneath an awning was a tidy row of plastic chairs, all with people waiting to enter the wards, more even sitting on the cold, hard ground. Everyone seemed tacitly well mannered and didn't make eye contact as they stared into space or kept their head down to read a book. None of them looked sick, and in fact they had rather rosy complexions, stronger and healthier than the people I saw on the streets or on public transport. It occurred to me that most of these people weren't sick at all. Since the passing of the Conjoinment Act, individuals who were of age had to get checkups at the hospital to assess the length of their window for conjoinment surgery. If they decided to get surgery beyond their date, they would have to bear all the risks and consequences. The income from these checkups and the surgeries helped the hospital pay off its bank loans for purchasing the land, the church building, and its operating costs. Which was to say, as long as we agreed to wound our bodies, we prevented this hill from being flattened. Having come to this thought, I couldn't help but feel joy.

I joined the line for checkups and inched closer to the consultation rooms. Two weeks ago, May helped me arrange a date and time for my full physical, the same way she saved me a seat in the lecture hall. She said I must get a thorough examination to see if my insomnia had any psychological or physiological impact or if it left lingering complications. I agreed without a fuss, hoping that my results would prove the effectiveness of sleep therapy to be overstated, that it offered no concrete help for those suffering from insomnia, so I could finally have a reason to stop going to those treatments, though not because I thought the sleep therapist lacked the skills to offer proper care.

After my last session, I'd gone on a bus and witnessed a dispute between a passenger and the bus driver about some incomprehensible issue. Clarity rose within my heart, and I understood what was happening to me and other people who couldn't sleep. The words May said penetrated my mind: *Everyone lives in their own world, but to avoid conflict, we fake companionship as if we're all kindred spirits.* People who suffer from insomnia or fluctuations in appetite, weight, and emotions are just those who have accidentally fallen through the cracks between their inner world and the external world. What we lack isn't balance, but the skill of disguise, preventing us from crossing that insurmountable distance. Once the driver chased that passenger off and the bus started moving again, I looked out the window and saw my impassiveness reflected in the glass. I thought about all the world's filth buried deep beneath the surface, how there is no need to unearth it, and how the cure for insomnia isn't to fix it, but to pretend that it doesn't exist at all. I don't know how I arrived at this conclusion—maybe it *was* the therapist's suggestive touch and words, but no one would be able to prove that.

Like fish, the polite patients filed into the examination rooms one after the other. I was part of the line, and following the nurse's instructions, I took off my dress and put on the thin gown the hospital provided. She measured my height, weight, and blood pressure. I let her pierce my fingertip to draw my blood, then I lay naked on a machine and let light puncture my organs. Once I finished my checkup, I sat with the people waiting for their results and watched the daylight slowly fade through the windows of the corridor, until the world outside was enveloped by a thick cloak of darkness, obscuring everything in view.

The hospital operated around the clock, so I had no way of knowing if the doctor sitting across from me had just started his shift or if he was about to go off duty. The only thing I was sure of was that his stiff and polite smile must be taught in professional etiquette courses for medical workers—it was the same kind of smile I saw on the faces of all the actors in the government's promotional videos.

"Hello." He nodded his head at me in greeting.

"Hello." I sat opposite him.

He flipped through the pages of my chart, and after an appropriately long pause, he looked up and said, "Your heart, lungs, kidneys, and liver are all working fine. You need to eat slower to prevent gas from bloating your stomach. Other than that, there are no abnormalities."

"But I've had insomnia for over six months..." I couldn't help but tell him.

"Insomnia is a common condition. It's not usually a serious problem," he said calmly. "Very few people sleep all the way through until morning."

"Is that something I should be comforted by?"

"You know, there's no such thing as immortality." He gave me a once-over. "A body that is strong and full of life could deteriorate the next second. You should hurry and get conjoinment surgery while there's still elasticity in your muscles and skin." He was earnest in his advice. "Otherwise, it'll be difficult for your wounds to heal. According to studies about life after conjoinment, the younger the subjects are when they complete surgery, the better their lives are, and they have fewer conflicts about sharing their bodies."

"After losing my sleeping routine, I feel like I've aged so quickly."

"That's not true, though." He glanced at my chart on his desk and assured me in a firm voice. "From now until winter of this year, your metabolic rate is still at the optimal level for conjoinment. But once winter is over, your body's functions will begin to deteriorate. You still have time," he said, and a smile spread across his face, as if he'd come across something worthy of delight.

The side exit of the hospital was on a slope with many gloomy-looking luxury residences up above. Below was a construction site where foundation work was being done, and woods so green they gleamed black. I took a left turn and went down a flight of steps made of stone, steep to the point of being almost vertical, and saw that the streets and shops the steps took me to were put together in strange ways. This wasn't an area I was familiar with, so I stopped every person who walked by me or paused for breath to ask if they knew where the bus stop was that would take me back to my university. But their answer was always the same: "I don't know."

I don't know. The way they said it made it sound like the university had never even existed. I walked to the next intersection and asked men and women holding groceries and with their children in tow for directions. They all either hesitated to speak or told me they were just as clueless about this place. I did a mental count of everyone I asked, and when the number of people who shook their heads at me reached thirty-six, I finally recognized the complicity in their faces and stopped feeling anxious, as if these voices that said they didn't know had helped me find a new direction.

⌣

I was going to call the sleep therapist and terminate my treatment with some made-up reason, but his nurse picked up the phone and said, "The next consultation will be on the hill next to our building," then she told me to wear a windbreaker. The thought of the cool breeze and that green hill, which I'd only ever seen through the window of the treatment room, plagued my mind. If location was tied to the development of my condition, I was curious about what the hill meant, and soon I heard myself saying "yes"—terminating all but forgotten.

There was a strong northeasterly wind on the morning of my appointment. I ran up the hill, and the therapist was already sitting on a red-and-white-checkered blanket.

Except for the lack of food, it looked like we were going on a picnic, the wind tugging our hair and the grass in the same direction.

He turned to me and said, "Hear how the wind passes by? There's a subtle rhythm that makes it sound like a certain piece of music. I don't know if you can hear it."

I saw his fingers drumming on the mat and understood that he was testing the progress of my recovery. Disdain rose within me; I was still being treated like a patient. "My sleep is no longer an issue." I told him that I had to make an important decision before winter ended, like so many others who had come of age in the city, and that my condition was normal for a person facing a dilemma— some people went to the hospital and got a new face, some left the town where they were born and never went back, and some threw large pieces of furniture out the window one by one, smashing cars and the heads of strangers.

"To me, sleep disorders are just types of self-regulation," I said.

"What's the decision that you have to make?" He fixed his gaze on me, his eyes as intense behind his glasses as piercing rays of light.

I told him that it was a decision about connecting my body to a body I'd never touched before.

"And how would you choose?" He looked rapt with curiosity.

"I don't know," I answered. "My choice probably has nothing to do with sleep."

"No," he said, in a tone that was incontestable. "It has everything to do with sleep." He smiled, and his smug expression triggered an inexplicable anger in me.

"How do you know?" I couldn't stop my voice from rising.

"You still don't know who I am?" he asked, incredulous.

"You're a therapist." Apart from that, I couldn't think of him in any other capacity.

The conceitedness of his smile spread to the rest of his face like a growing whirlpool, and I felt that it was something I had to fight against and win, but that bottomless body of water was capable of absorbing all my strength.

"Come." He pointed to the space beside him and said, softly, "Lie down; we'll start our last session."

He was speaking in a way therapists often do. I was sore in my knees and shoulders, and lethargy enshrouded me like fog. I settled my body on the mat, which was soft as a cloud, and took in the sharp, green scent of grass all around. The sky was bright as a knife's edge, so I shut my eyes, and just as I was about to lose consciousness, I heard him say, "You still don't know who I am."

He took my right hand and pressed my palm to his windbreaker. I could feel his warmth through the nylon, and underneath his flesh was a strong, steady pulse of something that reminded me of animals squirming in the soil before a formidable earthquake.

"Sometimes, people can't see with their eyes or listen with their ears. They must feel, like the blind."

I felt extra weight pushing down on my chest, the presence of a warm hand right above my heart like a problem with no solution, a kind of sadness that would never go away.

"Let me tell you my name." The cadence of his words matched his heartbeat, as though he was playing an instrument and singing at the same time. "It's Lok," he said. "Not 'Nok' as in music, the sounds people use to numb their emotions, but happiness."

Before I could react, his words shredded the film that separated me and him like barbed thorns. The fishy smell of the restaurant, the murmuring of the water tanks, the tropical fish with ghastly faces, the man my body was matched with, whose face I had forgotten—these moments surged through my sea of memories like whales racing to strand themselves on land.

All I could think of was how May had booked this sleep therapy on my behalf, and how this therapist had referred me for a checkup. Every single recommendation and action pointing toward one clear goal. I imagined these people towering above me, watching me as I crashed into wall after wall of my own maze, and felt the beat of my bewildered heart turn quick and erratic.

A frightening thought rose within me. *This is all a scam.* But to feign ignorance to the hand on my chest, I pulled all trains of thought to a halt and made my mind go blank.

"A match where two bodies are proven to be perfectly compatible is one in a million." His speech was raspy and hypnotic as he voiced his persuasions. "Once you attach your body to mine, your insomnia will disappear. No one loses sleep joined to a sleep therapist."

A long silence ensued; he seemed to be waiting for my response.

"You don't have to say yes immediately. You can think about it, but consider it well," he said eventually, as if he understood my lack of words.

To feign slumber, I tried my best to fall into unconsciousness, but spent too long drifting between vigilance and almost sleeping. A cool wind swept over me, flaking my skin into countless pieces that flew away through the air.

◡

The corridor of the dormitory was empty. There were no students in any of the rooms, no echoes of people talking. May hadn't left a note. The air was stagnant, filled with dust. I didn't open the window or turn on the lights. In the building opposite, people were moving shadows, drifting from window to window in their rooms, then to the corners near the stairs before receding to places farther within. Above the building was a sky sliced through by light. Occasional thick clouds floated by, casting dense gloom on the ground. The afternoon oscillated between light and dark; I lay on the bed, which was slightly damp, and imagined May standing in front of me. In my heart, I asked her why she felt she had to lure me into this situation.

"This is all a scam," I said.

"Is there anybody who isn't living a lie?" She would try to find the right words to explain herself. "The difference is in who tells the lie."

I knew there was no room for me to argue. Not because I lacked the ability to respond, but because she would be sure to caress my head and reassure me, saying that in life, it was impossible for anyone to differentiate between truths and untruths. "People who live a stable life in this city don't have any unique talents. They're just more compliant and good at developing firm beliefs," she would say as she looked at my face.

As the room grew darker, I became less and less sure if those were May's thoughts or another voice hidden within my body that was desperate to be heard. Even as the room sunk into pitch blackness, I still waited for May to return so I could tell her what my therapist had proposed and to say goodbye. Once I joined my body with his, I could no longer see myself living in this room. The voice I used to speak with her would change, and so would my posture as I lay on my bed. But there were no footsteps outside. The room was no different from an abandoned cardboard box. I looked up at the sky through the window. After what seemed like an eternity, it turned back into the white bleakness of day, and I had no choice but to concede that it was pointless to wait.

Once I agreed to the surgery, I discovered a disconcertingly joyous side of the city. With much misery and doubt, I told everyone I could think of about my decision, and every time, I saw their clouded expressions bloom like the sun, their mouths split into smiles and eyes shining a rare brilliance. Even though that brilliance quickly faded—it must have had something to do with how perplexed I looked and acted—they still shared my news among themselves, putting together a team and excitedly corresponding to prepare all the arrangements for the occasion, deciding on what balloons, flowers, beer, and vodka to buy, as if my surgery was a cause for celebration.

Although these things were no help at all to someone recovering from surgery, their high spirits made it hard for me to reject them. The only reason Lok had asked me to announce the date of our surgery was, in his words, to "save people the embarrassment of being surprised when they bump into you on a street or at a get together, only to see a person they've never met growing out of your body," so their enthusiasm was truly beyond my expectations. However, their excessive joy wasn't because their lives were boring—in a government leaflet about conjoined life, a psychiatrist advised all citizens to practice giving encouraging eye contact and accepting smiles. Everyone's appearance was part of the scenery of life, and people both pre- and post-surgery were more susceptible to external stimuli that could influence how they saw themselves.

"Pay attention to your expressions; you can help Reborns adapt to their new bodies, reducing the risk of infection or other complications," the psychiatrist recommended, also coining the name for people who consented to conjoinment as "Reborns."

My mother sent me several new sets of clothes in anticipation of my conjoinment. Two weeks before the surgery, Lok and I visited her in her apartment. We stood in front of the mirror together, obediently letting her wrap a measuring tape around our necks, shoulders, arms, waists, and legs. The afternoon sun crawled across my face and into my eyes, blunting my vision with sharp pain, and in that moment, I couldn't distinguish Lok from my mother, as if both of them were going to be wearing the set with me. As I turned my head toward a darker place in the room to rest my eyes, my mother sat down at the sewing machine, humming a happy tune while she cut the fabric, and it was like she wasn't working a pair of scissors or the machine, but a piano, the way Lok played music on my body. The sight of her was so familiar, her expression so similar to everyone else's who knew we were going to get conjoined, it shocked me into realizing that I wasn't just connecting my body with Lok, but with that disconcerting, unbridled joy. I had no idea where it would lead me, but I no longer had room for regret.

If by chance a tourist, someone not from here, came to the hospital, they would see a ward decorated like a party room, filled to the brim with ribbons and fairy lights, and think the people in this city must be simple and content with life, so much so that they get excited over blood and wounds. But even if this tourist existed, I couldn't be sure that their impression was necessarily false—no one could ever know if reality is just a mirage, refracted from the fragments of many other illusions.

Two days before the surgery, a nurse called and reminded me that I shouldn't eat for twelve hours before the operation and no water for six hours before. "To ensure your stomach is empty," she said. Then she added in a whisper, "Ideally, your mind should be empty, too. Leave everything behind; think about nothing at all. If you can, move into a new apartment for a while and forget everything about the past and your past self."

Although she spoke quietly, I still made out the self-satisfaction in her voice when she said, "Only then will you have enough space to take in another person's emotions and habits, reducing the chance of conflict—none of the guides about conjoinment will tell you this; it's all from my own experience and observations."

I hung up and continued thinking about what she said, but couldn't figure out how I could possibly put it into practice.

Then came the morning of the operation. I woke up feeling like my body had been hollowed out, untethered from the outside world. The despondent sky and wet wind, the fierce faces of people walking past, and the noise of street cleaners penetrated me like they would a shadow without leaving a single trace. I was an appliance unplugged from power, reacting to things on autopilot using the memory of my daily routine.

Wearing purple scrubs provided by the hospital, Lok and I walked past another ward, and the buzz of the crowd inside caught our attention. In each conjoinment surgery ward, the hospital reserved some of the rooms as living space for people who had just gotten sewn together, where they could stay until their wounds healed and where their family and friends could celebrate. We looked through the doorway and saw people we recognized talking and holding flutes of champagne, and knew that they had come for us. I waved enthusiastically at them, and they turned and called out my name. Just when I was about to head into the room and greet these people, a nurse grabbed me by the shoulders and gave me a look that said that wasn't where the surgery took place. So I followed the nurse and Lok and continued walking. Toward the end of the corridor, I could still hear the crowd cheer but couldn't understand why they were so excited. After thinking about it for a while, I recognized that they weren't cheering for us but for themselves: us becoming part of the conjoinment population was an encouragement that strengthened their beliefs and validated their own choices. I'd been swept up in their triumph and couldn't help but laugh.

In our consultation with the doctor, Lok made it clear that we wanted to be joined at our chests—to have the laceration there to connect our skin, soft tissue, and blood vessels. "My heart must be within her reach so it can soothe her while she sleeps," he explained, adding that we would accept no other arrangement. There were many other patients waiting outside, and the doctor spoke quicker and quicker about how our surgery was relatively simple and low risk. Once the operation was complete, we would look like a butterfly with different-shaped wings.

When we entered the operating room, the lead surgeon and a lawyer were already dressed in sterile suits, standing solemnly as if preparing for some kind of disaster. We lay down on the operating table. Before putting on gloves, the surgeon asked us a series of health questions I didn't understand, so I just nodded or shook my head when I needed to. Then the lawyer came over and read out a litany of long sentences to inform us that when we woke again, we will have forfeited our original identities to become part of a new individual with a new name, and that we were responsible for our decisions and actions. We offered our consent. Then another doctor approached, injected anesthetic into our arms, and asked us to count down from ten.

I descended into a black hole. There, time and weight didn't exist.

When I regained consciousness, we were being wheeled into a loud room. My entire body writhed with so much pain I couldn't open my eyes, but I could still hear people speak.

"This kind of union requires no sacrifice from either side, it looks so hasty, it's meaningless," someone commented.

"That's the way it is with the youth nowadays," another said.

I thought back to the lawyer's face and his disdain as he reluctantly did his work. Luckily, the anesthetic hadn't worn off completely, so we were still in a stupor. I kept my eyes shut and retreated back into the warm darkness.

When I woke again, there was only the faint sound of breath. I saw the tape on my arm securing an IV drip. May sat next to a dim yellow lamp, her head hung low. She wasn't alone—a man in a gray windbreaker was beside her on the couch, his chest against hers. He looked to be fast asleep and had his head resting on her shoulder. It occurred to me that this might be why May had disappeared, or maybe I was the one to disappear first, and in that time, this man had seized his chance to take up the space I'd left. Besides sleep, I knew then that I'd lost something even more important.

I was wrapped in layers of gauze and couldn't see what Lok and I looked like, but from May and that man's silhouette, I could clearly imagine how strange we appeared. Maybe it was the light, or my wounds, but I started to cry, thinking of the days when I first had trouble sleeping. Once everyone who had come to visit our dorm room left, only May remained, sitting in a chair next to my bed, a cigarette in her hand. Tonight, she wasn't holding a cigarette, but a book.

She glanced at me and put the book down. "Don't cry," she said. "There's no reason to cry." For a very long time, we didn't speak, and fixed our gazes on one spot in the ill-lit room.

Gradually, my eyes dried like the shriveled wings of a dead moth. Then I heard her voice, feeble as though coming from far away: "There's no need to be afraid. In this city, everyone must experience loss through necessary sacrifice. This is how we make this place better, to guarantee our lives. You don't need to worry that it's a bad decision, because it's not a decision, but an obligation. Everyone else our age has already experienced loss, whether or not they can bear it. What right do we have to demand that we live as our whole selves?"

I don't know when I stopped hearing her; I probably fell back asleep before her last sentence, so I have no idea when she left.

I woke again, and this time, blinding white sunlight poured into every corner of the room, so bright it might drown me and Lok to death. The nurse on duty saw me. "You're awake," she said, sounding pleasantly surprised. She propped me up, supporting my head and giving me a sip of water, then she went to the other side of the bed to check on Lok. "He's still asleep. Only a few lucky people stay out that long. When he wakes, everything in the past will no longer matter, and he'll be born again."

I studied his face. His skin was radiant with rest and emanated an aura I'd never seen before; indeed, he was like a newborn child. I was reminded of the dissertation I hadn't dared to work on when I was suffering from insomnia. Like a person who had been deprived of sensation, but could now feel the temperature of the room again, I asked the nurse for pen and paper and resumed my writing.

Every sleep is, in fact, a temporary death. Only after experiencing these short deaths over and over can we acclimatize to the various conditions of our existence.

Case Study I

**The Ceremony of Physical Separation: Elisa C.
Johansson / Melina Johansson**

Once Elisa was separated from her sister Melina, the left side of her face and body started to wither away slowly, like a cut piece of a plant. Every day when she woke, half of her would be spent, haggard, while the other half was vivacious and flourishing. This was why Elisa couldn't bear to see herself in a mirror. She had thought that separation surgery would give her a new, wonderful life, but her diaries and letters, made public for research after her passing, showed that she always seemed to be at a loss. She wrote, *I just want to find a place where I can hide and seal myself away and never be found by anyone.* Evidently, her asymmetrical body was a source of shame. If appearance and physique were things one could forge, to Elisa any attempt was like trying to mold water. Her body was never within her control, neither before nor after her surgery.

Elisa's aversion to mirrors did not come from a fixed notion of beauty, but because she could see Melina in her reflection and witness her growth and change. She always sensed Melina's presence, but the woman in the mirror looked so corporeal and alive, Elisa had no way of escaping her.

She never again touched Melina's body after the surgery. When she woke, the doctor shined a light into Elisa's eyes to check her pupils, then told her that her sister was resting in another room but was in poor condition. A few days later, a nurse bringing Elisa food informed her that Melina had developed a fever after the operation and had passed away the night before. Apparently, Elisa remained impassive throughout, displaying no shock or sorrow, and continued to eat in silence, her eyes wide. Dr Robert Smith, the surgeon who operated on the Johansson sisters, and who wrote about Elisa and Melina's case in his book *Fated Bodies: Conjoinment and Civil Rights*, describes Elisa's reaction to Melina's death as cold and indifferent, "as if she was informed of the death of a complete stranger." From that, he claims conjoined twins are adversaries from the moment they are conceived. Their antagonistic relationship only grows with age as they continuously compete for nutrients, survival, attention, identity, talent, and dominance, even limbs, intentionally or otherwise. Therefore, the only thing that can grow between two bodies where distance is impossible is hatred.

Elisa's opinions were only ever documented in the interview collection *Betrayed Bodies: Conjoinment and the Obstacles of Daily Life*, where she admitted that her time conjoined with Melina were the darkest days of her life. When they lay in bed, neither one of them could sleep because they could never agree on which side to turn. They argued day and night, and even when they stopped, their silence bristled with negativity. The only thing they agreed upon was their desire to split from each other, and to this goal, they were each willing to make concessions to get their own bodies, though their motivations for separation were different. Melina was always anxious and vocal about her nightmares of dying on the operating table, but Elisa's fantasies of freedom became more and more concrete until they were practically real. In the interview, Elisa recounted Melina's words, mimicking her sister's tone and demeanor: "No matter the result, even if the surgery kills us, I still want us to get into the operating room as soon as we can; at least then my body will stop shaking."

Maybe Melina was right, Elisa thought. Once the surgery was done, they would have to face death—even if their hearts continued to beat, their identity as conjoined twins, the only form they had known, which was intrinsic to their existence and their values, would be no more, and the world that opened itself before them, where they were but frail individuals, was as unfathomable as death. Melina manifested her premonition and died from complications six days after the operation. To Elisa, the outcome was entirely unsurprising, and not for a lack of sisterly affection for Melina. In fact, they loved each other very deeply; it was just that their flesh was so tightly bound, they never found the right ways to express compassion for one another. Elisa had long prepared herself for solitude, and she had mustered enough courage to face their separation, whether that came to them as two independent and flawed bodies, or in the polar states of life and death.

The way Elisa saw it, she survived not because she was physically stronger or was optimistic, as the medical staff and reporters inferred. She had merely been assigned to stay in the place of the living, whereas Melina was sent to another world to continue her life. That was how she understood their separation. In Elisa's view, she and Melina were two souls that happened to enter a connected pair of bodies, and their separation only meant that they were returning to the places they each belonged. Allegorically, she described herself as being on one side of the mirror, and Melina on the other—and nobody could tell which side was real and which side was the reflection. This was how she interpreted life and death. "To Melina, I must also have passed away," Elisa said.

Sometimes, when she looked into the mirror and scrutinized what was there to see, Elisa would spot Melina and realize she had grown taller just like her, her features also deepening as they stepped into puberty together and experienced the same bewilderments. They no longer insisted on their own points of view for every trivial thing, becoming taciturn teenage girls with bodies that weighed them down more than before. After the departure of their conjoined sister, their solitary body had to carry the temperaments, preferences, habits, principles, and misalignments of at least two people. As the fortuitous survivor of the operation, Elisa felt the most far-reaching and incurable repercussion had to be Melina's quirks seeping into her soul. After the success of the surgery, all the fierce disputes, the conflicts, and the hurt they had inflicted on each other, so tangible in the past, became incommunicable, though Elisa had no intention of asking anyone for help. Having spent a good chunk of her childhood in hospital, she understood on a visceral level that not disclosing pain was the way to avoid having to endure more tests and physical torture.

"Doctors are excitable; they want to help even if it's something beyond their ability. Doctors are also curious and want to learn more about the secrets of the human body, so they always end up solving nothing and leaving more wounds on the bodies of their patients," Elisa explained in her interview.

Yet, the conflicts that became internal were not as intangible as Elisa claimed. Once she reached puberty, she found the left side of her body starting to droop; she had a bacterial infection in some of her nerves, and half of her body was afflicted with muscular paralysis.

"A side of me has already lost sensation." Elisa was middle-aged when she was interviewed, and her hemiplegia had immobilized the left side of her body and face. "I thought I was being seized by Melina. Or was my right side her all along? I don't know."

Elisa said she often fainted on the street, especially on days the air was thick with pollution. But when she regained consciousness, she always found herself lying in the comfort of her couch at home. There were more people willing to lend a helping hand than she expected, and this was puzzling to her. One of them was Judd, who ended up becoming her husband.

Their neighbors, family, and friends, the master of ceremonies, everyone who witnessed their relationship come together, thought Judd took Elisa's hand out of pity and that Elisa was a lucky woman. People often assumed conjoined people could not stand solitude and easily attached themselves to other people. However, Judd insisted he was always mesmerized by the way Elisa looked; in fact he could hardly take his eyes off her. She reminded him of a sun shower, rain on one side and sunshine on the other, as if he were standing between light and darkness. The first time he met her, she was unconscious beside a flower bush in a park. He shook her awake, and as he escorted her home, he took his time studying her face, admiring the changes in her expressions, every quiver an asymmetrical motion that rippled across her features. Even after he bid her goodbye, her face kept shifting in his mind.

In his interview, Judd declared his love for Elisa, incomprehensible to many. As she grew older, she got thinner, making the sag of her left side more severe. Every morning when he had breakfast, Judd would stare at his wife, busy in the kitchen, and sink into his fantasies—she was an iron tower, leaning more toward him every year, and he was a tourist at the attraction, taking photos to commemorate his visit. Always, after a long time, he would be brought back to reality and carry on eating, sometimes feeling deeply guilty for not empathizing enough with the pain his wife's deformity caused her.

"I've never been able to fantasize about another person as much as I did with Elisa." Judd said those fantasies were enough for him to forget the many distresses of life. Elisa was also a source of distress at times, but one he took pleasure in, even developing an inextricable need for as time went on.

In their many years of marriage, Judd was never sure if he would wake up in bed one morning next to a different person. He was convinced his wife was really a rotation of several similar-looking women with vastly different personalities, but even if he caught them in their act, he wouldn't have any evidence with which to expose them.

"Just before her period, she would have cravings and become irritable, sharp-tongued but depressed," he said, but denied that it was an effect of her menstruation. He and their two sons were used to her mercurial moods. Even on days when she was well rested, her face was like a sky indecisive about its weather, changing shades in an instant, often frightening the children, until they eventually got used to a panic-stricken life.

Elisa always thought she was easiest on her younger son, who had a learning disability. "Everyone is born with talent; they're just talented at different sorts of things," she said to the journalist. Her son agreed, saying that his mother was so keen on discovering his unique skills that her obsession caused him to feel ashamed of himself, like he was barren soil where nothing could grow.

"She would sometimes shout at me all of a sudden for not being born talented or for not trying hard enough to make up for what I lack." Speaking in a mumble, the son also admitted the fear he had of his mother, especially when she acted like the authorities she often complained about, who oppressed people who were different. But throughout the interview, he emphasized that she was most often a gentle and caring mother, and always made him his favorite carrot dishes on holidays.

"Sometimes, the way she watched over me seemed to be less like protectiveness for a child and more like the possessiveness for a lover," he said. His mother had always been hostile toward his lovers, even though she kept stressing that romance was the best spice for a dull life. When the son grew up, he became a man who was sensitive and empathic, adept at telling the moods of other people.

Judd also said Elisa was a jealous wife; she liked to check his phone calls and emails in secret, and demanded he describe in detail the appearances and personalities of every single person he met or was acquainted with. "She just needs to know everything, to have all the information within her grasp." With a note of resignation, he recounted how she once asked him to find a pretty woman to start an affair. "She even gave me advice on how to choose a partner," he said, adding that she felt an affair would not only enliven their weary marriage, but also offer her respite so she could set aside her roles as a wife and a mother.

On the tenth visit to their house, the interviewer implored Judd to talk about the secret sides of Elisa so that the story could be more accurate, at which Judd finally relented and revealed details of their intimate life. In their cramped, almost claustrophobic home, Elisa would close the flimsy wooden door of their bedroom, role play different characters, and ask Judd to be her audience. "She always wanted me to treat her like a veteran prostitute; that's one of the roles she was most fascinated by."

Some of the characters she played had a complex backstory, like an assassin or a CIA agent, but she was most often a nurse, a cleaning woman, a prison warden, or a divorcee, imploring him to join her in her fantasies. Judd didn't find roleplay arousing at all. Instead, he took it as a sign that she was exhausted with her life, to the point where she had to release the divided selves hidden deep within her.

Judd believed Melina still existed, even though he had never met her. But every time he felt lost in Elisa's unpredictable moods, he would comfort himself by thinking that the woman before him was really Melina and not his wife. Gradually, he even started to doubt himself—maybe he had been bewitched by Melina all along, not Elisa.

Judd's worries were not entirely excessive or baseless. Early in his life, Carl Jung also said that he possessed two personalities: No. 1 was the conscious ego; No. 2 was the inner self. They were polar opposites yet coexisted, the result of every individual splitting their selves over the course of their lives. Similarly, for Elisa and Melina, they had separate minds, so their inner selves split at different stages of growth even though their bodies were connected. This may have bewildered Judd, but it is a condition that occurs in everyone—not just conjoined people—including Judd himself, only that he had been unaware.

To Elisa, it was obvious that her husband had multiple personalities. From the moment he woke up in the morning to when he stepped out the door, Judd was a doting and considerate husband, rising earlier than Elisa to make breakfast so she could sleep in a little longer. She could hear him sing to himself as he fried eggs and warmed the milk like a cheerful, optimistic person. Once they finished breakfast, he would kiss her before leaving the house instead of saying goodbye, but she knew the person who came back through the same door at sunset would be the husband who frightened her, raging against the office air and his chair and his colleagues, how much he disliked the taste of the food she had made. Sometimes, he reeked of alcohol and vomit, and beat her and their sons for no reason at all.

And then, when he woke up the next morning and saw their bruises, he would cry and beg for forgiveness. To show just how remorseful he was, he would hit himself with a wooden stick until he had bruises of about the same sizes as the ones he had inflicted on them. Elisa paid little attention to his apologies, knowing this would happen all over again like an inevitable cycle. The one thing she found intriguing was Judd's violent reaction when she suggested that he find himself a mistress. Not only did he scream that she was insane, he slapped a hand over her mouth to stop her from saying anything else. "This shows how terrified he was of the desire in his heart; he was desperate to stop that part of him from growing," she stated emphatically.

Through the case of Elisa and Judd, it can be seen that the self proliferates as incessantly as mold. Every individual is also a multitude of selves, no matter if they are born conjoined or as a singular body. Once the multiplicity of Elisa met the multiplicity of Judd, they connected, fought, broke apart, and reconciled, supporting and harming one another. Their many selves also gave space for them to take a breath and withdraw from each other; if they ended up loathing their partner, all they had to do was fall in love with another of their partner's selves. This was why Elisa and Judd could still live under the same roof and under a contract society had approved, and in this sense, they were a more fortunate pair than Melina and Elisa.

Slant

Lok's body was a cold, disused pipe, where time was still.

This was a thought exercise from *The Conjoinment Manual*, in the section "Notes for Reborns," for people who had undergone conjoinment surgery less than three months ago. According to the manual, thought exercises were just as important as the physiotherapy sessions we were to attend three times a week.

In the first stage of postoperative recovery, many patients fall into a state of body confusion from the conjoinment of foreign flesh to their own. Early symptoms include an inability to identify with the body with which one is connected—even perceiving that mass to be no different than cold, large rock—and a tendency to instigate conflict. In more severe cases, Reborns may feel that their own existence is threatened. It is advisable to do thought exercises at least once a day to prevent these complications.

To do a thought exercise, close your eyes, take a deep breath, and relax your muscles. Let your favorite things emerge in your mind. Associate the shapes and features of these things with your partner, and transfer your feelings of pleasure onto them. To accept a new body, you must start with your mind.

Lok and I woke up in bed at different times, but every morning, we would still do a thought exercise together with our eyes closed from the manual like pious believers. I tried my best to associate him with harps, sculptures, fences, and abandoned teddy bears. As sunlight came in through the window and crept up the bed, I imagined he was a banyan tree: I was trying to avoid getting dark spots on my skin, I was hiding in his shade. We never told each other what we'd conjured for each other, as if to preserve a few remaining secrets for ourselves.

But perhaps it was a time when we shouldn't even have had the luxury of secrets. Although we were still living at the same place as before the surgery—it was in a familiar neighborhood, after all, where we were both born and raised—our changed physical form turned everyday life into a series of confusions. I had read the cautionary advice in *The Conjoinment Manual*, but it was still frustrating to experience it for myself, like when we opened a door to enter a room, but smashed the other person into the door frame, or when one of us tripped on the street, making the other fall too, and then it was a struggle to get back up. If one of us turned right, the other would think we had to go left to arrive at our destination. Since the manual advised that we should "always be patient, always be courteous, lest conflict become the cause of ruin," we ended up paralyzed before traffic lights, neither one of us willing to articulate what we truly thought, instead vying to be the one to conform (or really, we each just wanted to avoid the responsibility of being in the wrong). Having sore feet when the other still hadn't had enough of a walk, going to a concert when the other was nodding off to sleep… These countless contradictions tore invisible fractures in the environment we'd grown accustomed to, and if we so much as let our guard down, we would fall through these cracks into the dark even as the wound on our chests slowly scabbed over.

Our doctor not only agreed with us, but he was also further evidence of our difficulties. Every month, we visited his clinic and lay on a white bed as he examined our body and probed us with sharp tools to make sure nothing was out of the ordinary with our recovery. I was on my back, staring at the doctor's knitted brows as he concentrated on his work, noticing the way he spread himself toward us while the woman joined with him, wearing a shapely suit, tried her best to angle her body and head to the side, as if she didn't see us, to give us our dignity as patients. Or this was what I'd assumed at first—after making a few calls to her subordinates and sending some emails on her laptop, the woman stared at a black bird perched outside the window, lost in thought, and it was then that I realized she seemed to be in a different world altogether, even though her body was connected to another person's. I had the impression that she was a human outgrowth protruding from the doctor's physical boundaries, or that he was a newborn blossomed from her body. Every time he moved, she had no choice but to coordinate herself to match; they acted like the two wings of an enormous insect with no central thorax, so their movements were never perfectly aligned.

When the examination was complete, the doctor warned us, as he always did, "Don't hold onto any negative feelings toward your new body. Once you start complaining and it becomes a habit, no medicine can treat your negativity. There aren't many cases of successful separations. Even if we're able to, there would be a heavy price to pay." His tone reminded us of a distant relative or friend who bombards a reunion with their troubles in life, or maybe this was his tactic for getting us to leave, so we just nodded, lips pursed without another word.

This was how we took pleasure in our appointments each and every time—the doctor and his conjoined partner were in the same predicament as we were, and we delighted in their company.

"Their disunity originates from their decision to remain in their jobs rather than working together." Sometimes, Lok treated the doctor as his own patient, analyzing his situation even though he would never have the chance to prescribe a remedy. Perhaps he was also dropping a careful hint to me, only I couldn't catch his implication in the moment. It was a busy time; we were like two infants newly arrived in the world, relearning all kinds of life skills. We trained our weak and scrawny body and learned to walk and run in sync, how to get into and out of vehicles, how to allocate our limited time—after all, we were a pair of joined bodies, but still had the work of two people to complete before day's end.

Not long after surgery, we sat before our desk, a custom-made one for conjoined people, and wrote down a list of things we could each let go of. I applied to distribute my remaining credits at the university to courses that allowed distance learning, having only my dissertation left to complete, while he shortened the hours at his clinic. I hardly went out with my friends anymore, nor did I speak much with them, and he no longer missed the patients who had already recovered. To preserve what little freedom we had from each other, we increased the time we each spent unconscious. With one small look, one of us would get the message and swallow a sleeping pill. As time went by, however, the pills became less effective, and I often resorted to closing my eyes and stiffening my body, letting my mind wander astray.

It would be impossible to list out all the tedious details of our routine, but we got up, washed, ate, drank, and used the bathroom together, finishing our tasks at around the same pace. Lok said, "Cultivating discipline means setting limits for yourself and focusing on what's important." To my mind, though, it was a way to suppress our wants before they spilled over into dangerous, forbidden territory—not only physical desire, but also the desires emerging from the dark corners of our hearts.

Once our wound healed, our habits were even more in sync. We often sat on a small couch in the café next to the park, watching people walk by outside the full-length windows. Sometimes we counted the people passing by who were conjoined, taking turns to point out the habits of each pair and guess how long they had been sewn together. I'd never realized the conjoined population had increased so much so quickly and began to feel a sense of unreality. I knew very well that life before conjoinment was already disintegrating, but the world after conjoinment seemed like it was still being solidified, and should a formidable wind come, everything around us would be blown back to its original state.

Lok thought nothing of my worries. "Life is stagnant and meaningless if we don't discover even the slightest change in ourselves each day." This, to him, was the spirit of conjoinment. I only smiled in resignation; I don't know when I'd started to lose my will and zest for arguing. Perhaps at some point, in a moment of inadvertent insight, I learned that it was a trait people disliked. To adapt to this mutually restrictive body, we affected gentle habits, like the way I suddenly developed an addiction to coffee and found the bitter, brown drink to have an intriguing, sweet aroma. Lok was similarly obsessed; once we had several cups, we would politely touch each other's lips with our own, not minding the residual sour taste in our mouths. Much later, I came to recognize the dregs of anxiety accumulating little by little in my subconscious. If volatility and change are intrinsic to life, everything that happens passes in the next moment, and that was how the tranquil harmony of our early days of conjoinment came to an end.

We couldn't pinpoint when the first rash slithered up our skin, only that one morning, I was the first to wake, and felt an itch in the part that connected us. I scratched with my nails and discovered small, red bumps in the recess where my body overlapped with his. On subsequent mornings, I opened my eyes earlier and earlier, staring at the cluster of rashes, hoping they would go away, or at least stay within a confined area so we could dismiss it as some kind of allergy. But it didn't go away. In fact it got worse, and spread beyond the shade of our recess into broad daylight.

We could no longer pretend that the rash didn't exist. Finally, as we were taking a shower, Lok said, "This isn't a typical skin condition."

I kept my face blank and said, "We need a doctor's diagnosis." He stopped talking to me after that, and I avoided meeting his eyes. We dried off and immediately called the hospital to request an earlier checkup. But it was peak season, and the nurse on the line told us that even if our symptoms were severe, it would still take two weeks to get an appointment. When we hung up, our apartment was suddenly suffocating, as if covered in a layer of smoke. I avoided Lok's gaze, but I could guess what his eyes would convey. He must think that I was the source of the inflammation, and though I couldn't figure out why, I also considered it to be my fault. Soon, the rash between us grew into a shapeless wall.

As we waited for our checkup, I never stopped thinking about the rash and why it might have appeared. While I wallowed in my thoughts, I recalled the days I'd spent in Lok's clinic, with Lok in his white coat and me wearing my favorite clothes. To extricate myself from his business, I'd twisted my body in the opposite direction as much as I could, headphones blasting music to separate myself from the space Lok shared with his patients.

Once we connect our bodies with another person, we inevitably become a bystander to their lives. This sentence surfaced in my mind one afternoon as I accompanied Lok to work, and I wrote it down on a notepad as material for my dissertation. Before, I'd always brought a book with me, but now I preferred to just close my eyes. There, I was in an ocean. I was floating and coming across things that had been left behind at different times and places, and they were all covered in dust—like Professor Foot's response to me. After getting my surgery, I'd sent him an email describing my wound, to which he simply replied, *Your research has just begun*. I didn't understand what he meant at the time. It was only when I sat in Lok's clinic that I heard the impatience in his words: he was waiting for me to hand in my dissertation. With that, the time as I waited for Lok to finish his work became profound and meaningful. I ruminated in silence, gradually discovering all the subtle details I'd overlooked in my thesis argument. I could feel my whole being expanding from within, my inner world richer and fuller than it had ever been before I got conjoined.

Lok had no idea. He only saw how content I looked and smiled with relief, saying, "I'm glad you find my workplace comfortable." To his mind, in the near future I would also put on a white coat and become his assistant. I never tried to break the truth to him, harmony being worth more than sincerity.

One night, I thought of May again. Ever since her brief visit to my room that late night after my surgery, we no longer had deep or meaningful conversations and parted ways like casual acquaintances moving on with their lives. As I woke from my dream in shock, I realized how unbelievably estranged we had become. I looked at Lok's face for a while, making sure he was snoring and fast asleep, then I turned to make a phone call.

It only took a few rings before my call was answered. A woman's voice came through, still doused in sleep. "Who's this?"

Reluctantly, I told her my name.

"I couldn't tell it was you," she gasped, articulating my suspicions.

To dispel the awkwardness, I came up with an excuse: "It's probably because I've changed my daily routine." Then, lest she respond with annoyance, and to stop the unbearable silence that was mounting between us, I carried on with a question. "How's your dissertation going?"

She hesitated. "I don't remember anything about it." After getting conjoined, life had gotten so busy, she'd had to put the whole thing aside. There was disappointment in her voice, but I wasn't sure if it was for her poor memory, or if she might just be feeling disheartened about the messy state of her apartment.

Finally, she couldn't stay awake any longer and hung up. I stared vacantly at a corner of the wall where the paint was peeling, feeling that something had been irretrievably lost. I had no doubt that May was the person on the phone with me—she just wasn't the May I knew. The May who used to live with me, who I'd share my thoughts with every day, was gone without a trace, along with her dissertation, swallowed by an insuperable black hole. I seemed to be the only one who cared, though it mattered to no one else. Coldness settled in my heart, and I thought that, at some point unbeknownst to me, maybe a certain part of myself had also slipped away along with the core beliefs of my dissertation. I shifted my gaze to the darkened windows, waiting for daylight to pass through them. Soon, Lok would wake, rub his eyes, and take me to work. I'd sit on a chair, pretending to be immersed in music, even though I'd just be lost in my thoughts, in that vast ocean, trying to salvage people and things that had long since sunk to the bottom.

When Lok and I sat opposite the doctor and told him about our rash, I omitted my call with May and the thoughts that I'd had. Experience had taught me it was foolish to speak from the heart with doctors, so I only said how hard it'd been getting used to this new body while having to finish all the household chores with another person in tow. It was impossible to wash our sheets and curtains before they got infested with dust mites, which must be how we became vulnerable to the bacterial infection flourishing across our skin like wildflowers.

After I spoke, I realized that my words sounded more defensive than remorseful. The doctor looked at me, and

Lok also turned his head, their eyes burning holes on my skin. I felt like I was no longer in a clinic, but a closed court.

Eventually, Lok pulled his attention back to the doctor and asked, "How did this happen?"

The doctor reassured him, "You two have very different bodies, after all. Even though you had surgery only after a rigorous matching process, rejection is still an unavoidable phase. It's just that in your case, it happened far too early."

"Are these complications common?" Lok was still worried.

"Most symptoms of rejection and allergic reaction have psychological causes, like from a lack of confidence, or pessimism, or an unwillingness to submit." The doctor laid his gaze on my face again, and I had to lower my head.

He promised to give us a prescription for the inflammation, but told us that it would only alleviate our symptoms and wouldn't guarantee recovery.

We left the hospital at rush hour. People were pouring out of office buildings and swarming the streets like sand. At the taxi stand, conjoined people gathered on one side, and individuals waited in line on the opposite side. Only a few taxis stopped for the individuals, while a steady stream headed toward the conjoined passengers. Maybe the drivers were responding to the growth of the conjoined population, or maybe they'd modified their vehicles after their own surgeries. Apart from making room for larger bodies, they may have also changed the way they made a living, and only accepted passengers with the same physical condition.

We lined up, and after a long wait, stumbled into a taxi. Before the traffic light changed color, a man holding a briefcase walked past our car and gave us a look that seemed to be jealousy or resentment. I stared at his still-intact body until Lok said my name, tearing my thoughts away from the man.

Lok wanted to ask me what music I'd been listening to lately. I told him the name of a band; they were rather underground, but he actually knew them and said that every note they sang sounded like the cry of desperate souls.

"Their music is pure mawkish whining." He said it wasn't good for me to listen to that kind of music all the time. "Here, I made you a playlist," he said, and let the songs he picked addle the space inside my head.

"Rather than idling your time away waiting for me to get off work, it's better if you start learning how to be a clinic assistant." He said clinic assistants don't require university training, and I should be able to handle the job with ease. I kept agreeing with him until the taxi arrived at the building we lived in. The driver and his partner were scrutinizing Lok and me through the rearview mirror, so I became curious about Lok's face. Ever since we'd gotten sewn together, we had been confined to a fixed distance, unable to move farther away from or closer to each other. Even if I twisted my neck to the side until it hurt, I only ever saw the left side of his face, submerged in shadow.

Night fell, shrouding the entire city in black. Lok slept deeply, his breathing even and steady like endless washes of waves. I was festering with anxiety, feeling what little freedom I had left slipping through my fingers. I reached out to the bedside table to pick up my phone. But just as I started dialing, I thought about how calling couldn't lead me to May anymore. Although she was technically still May, the person I knew had already been metabolized, crumbled into some kind of detritus and faded away. Maybe this was a process everyone—Professor Foot, my mother, Bak, Lok, and me—had to go through. We had all involuntarily drifted apart from people we loved, so we each shared an equivalent solitude—we escaped from one kind of solitude, only to fall into yet another. I put down the phone and tried to speak with the May I knew. When we lived in the dormitory, she and I both knew that talking was just an act to make sure the other person's response would be close to what we expected, and so as time passed, we got closer even when we didn't open our mouths to speak.

I closed my eyes, and saw the May who no longer existed. She looked just as she always did, wearing a flamboyant yet depressing red outfit with wide sleeves, which made her body look even more slight. She'd folded herself into a corner of our room.

"I've been found out." I walked over and sat down next to her.

"Hm?" She raised her eyebrows.

"I've become my forgotten self again, but stronger, tougher, too."

"When did that happen?"

"When I first thought of the conclusion of my dissertation."

"That's all right. Our selves tend to grow and shed like hair when we least expect it. It's a process that happens over and over again." This was how she'd comfort me.

"But my selves are now in conflict with each other."

166

"Just close the wrong one off," she said. "You'll know which one that is."

I was reminded of the dog May used to have. It had light brown fur and was her most cherished friend. Whenever May went back home for the holidays, she must cuddle it to fall asleep, and they depended on each other's scent for comfort. But May's apartment was in a building where dogs were prohibited, so she had to tie her dog to its cage in the kitchen and teach it to guard its mouth so that it never barked and attracted the attention of prying neighbors. May told me that countless birds and pets lived in that building, and to survive, all of them had learned to silence their voices and hide away their bodies.

"Which one of my selves should I tame, and how?" I asked her.

"Which one do you wish to kill?" she asked back.

"Which one of them deserves to die?" I asked her.

⌣

Soon, daylight came, landing on Lok's face, tracing his features with a thin strand of gold. To store the sight in an unshakeable part of my mind, I lightened my breathing to delay his waking. When he finally opened his eyes, still glazed with sleep, I made my request: "I need a vacation."

"What?" he mumbled.

"Just a few days. To go back to living alone for a while."

"Haven't you always been on vacation?" His eyebrows furrowed like he was dealing with something bothersome. "You haven't even started working."

"I just need a few days," I pressed on. "Let me take care of a past matter by myself."

"And what would that be?" he asked.

I shook my head. "Something I'm trying to eliminate, to forget."

To deliberately forget is nonsensical, he said, but still he acquiesced to my plea. He agreed to take the sleeping pills regularly and close the clinic for a week as long as I gave him three hours of waking time each day to handle any essential business. Out of guilt or sympathy, I told him I really only needed five days.

⌣

As he'd promised, Lok fell into a deep slumber. His body relaxed like he was sinking to the bottom of the sea, weighing down on my right side until I could hardly support him. I lost my balance, and we both toppled onto the couch.

I slipped a cotton sleeping bag over him and strapped him tightly to my body with hooks and belts. He tipped into me like a collapsing hill. I could just manage to walk with the support of a metal cane, so I wasn't worried, since the path I had in front of me wasn't long. Even before he agreed to take the extra-strength sleeping pills, I had already completed my research on Aunt Myrtle, made an appointment with her over email, and copied the address in the notes app on my phone. This was going to be my last fieldwork excursion, and I knew I needed to complete it as quickly as possible. I didn't even have time to read up on Aunt Myrtle's organization, but I felt I already knew everything about her—she had lived in my memory for years, and although memory and fantasy are very similar things, her voice and figure were still so clear and palpable.

As I sat in the taxi carrying Lok and a tote bag, I could almost feel her breath and hear her footsteps. The taxi sped through the cross-harbor tunnel, driving past a stately, stone-cold funeral home and some abandoned industrial buildings before arriving in the city's poorest district. Here, tramps and beggars wandered the streets, and the dilapidated buildings were home to countless addicts, overstaying immigrants, old prostitutes, black-market workers, and asylum seekers with no legal right to work. Twenty years ago, my aunt established a charity offering consulting services and practical assistance to people seeking separation from their conjoined partners. At the top of the organization's website was its longtime mission—SEPARATION IS A BASIC HUMAN RIGHT. The office was located in a slanted building, which had been listed as dangerous for years but showed no sign of collapsing. Since no one was interested in demolishing or repairing the premises, the landlords rented out the units below market price. It was a place that had been abandoned, inhabited by people who had also been forgotten.

The taxi stopped right in front, then the driver looked at me and said, "Be careful with your luggage." Aunt Myrtle's office was on the fifth floor and the building didn't have an elevator. I carried Lok up the stairs without coming across anybody else. The stairwell stank of feces and rotten fruit, and I was struck with the image of Sisyphus rolling his boulder and all the world's futility up the hill. It gave me a small, ineffable solace— this certainty of failure regardless of my effort, and an outcome that seemed like nothing had taken place at all.

I dragged Lok to the metal gates outside the organization's office, my breath too rapid and erratic for speech, which worked out just fine to cover up my agitation when I made eye contact with the woman who opened the door. The skin around her eyes was loose, creased with fine lines and wrinkles and speckled with age spots. She wore a black-and-white striped dress and had only one arm, the empty sleeve swaying slightly. Her skin was the color of fruit peel left to dry in the sun for too long. In the dim yellow light, only her eyes, which shimmered with sadness, helped me to reconcile this freshly old woman with the young model who'd graced the covers of fashion magazines so many years ago.

"The stairs in this building are terribly long and the steps are intolerably steep," she said genially. Then she spotted Lok in the sleeping bag and frowned. "Isn't this supposed to be a couple's consultation?" Her voice turned taut and stern. "Separation must be a joint decision; you can't deceive the other person."

I quickly explained that I just wanted to learn about all the possible outcomes and the experiences of people who chose to separate, which were hard to come by. "No one knows what the future will bring," I said.

Breathing a sigh of defeat, she let me into the office, using her one hand to help me transport Lok over to the couch. "Healthy men, they weigh as much as fridges," she

grunted. By the time we were done, she was utterly exhausted too, and we all collapsed onto the thick cushions
of the couch. From my position, I noticed that the interior
of the office, the table, murals, crystal displays, windows
and the scenery they opened on, even her hairstyle, they
were all slightly tilted, making me wonder if it was just
an effect of the building being off-kilter or if I was losing
my center of gravity.

"The rent here must be affordable," I said to her.

"The price isn't the point." Aunt Myrtle glanced
at me as if to scoff at my question, then told me that
twenty years ago, when the city was still prosperous, this
district was so remote that other than a few children of
different ethnicities, the streets were empty the whole
day, like somewhere in outer space. When the real-estate
agent reluctantly brought her for a site visit, she could
hardly take her eyes off of this building that looked like
it was about to come crashing down. Every window was
dark, like rows of decayed teeth. There was also a large
fissure between two units that seemed to be widening,
and through that gap she could glimpse the next street.
It was then that she made up her mind to establish her
separation consultancy, which had just had its permit
approved, here in this building.

At the time, she was still supporting herself with crutches, her fresh amputation wound bundled up in white bandages. After she and the man she'd been conjoined with went their separate ways—they had been connected at the shoulder, and he left her with just the one arm—she was deprived of her longtime support and constantly lost her balance. She keeled over in shopping malls, cinemas, restaurants, and on train platforms like a tinkling glass bottle, and when people walked past, they would glance at her and look away, as if she was a piece of wastepaper or a plastic bag dropped on the ground.

"People don't mean it in a contemptuous or discriminatory way, nor do they bear any malice. It's just a habit to avoid people or things that might be a threat. No one likes to live constantly worrying about themselves," she said. She would get up from the floor and take her time looking into the faces of the people around her, trying to decipher the messages they each carried, and started to have a clear understanding of the human psyche.

The first time she laid her eyes on this wobbly-looking building, the building seemed to look right back at her, and she felt she'd found a kindred spirit to rely on. "Only people who have experienced loss or are on the verge of loss would identify with such a building." She came to this conclusion after considering her own feelings. "Especially that fissure—it makes them feel like this is a safe place to be." Once her organization was established, she came to sit in the small office every day, ready to bare her heart and share her experience with anyone who came seeking help. But so few people visited her office, she sometimes felt she'd been the only person ever to undergo separation surgery.

"Maybe people are deterred by the look of the building. It seems like it's going to collapse anytime," I said.

"But we're never going to avoid all the accidents that could happen in our lives," she insisted. "Once we recognize this, we can understand why that crack is as necessary to this building as the surgical wounds are to our bodies, and this decrepit district to the rest of the city."

As early as adolescence, when her body was quickly changing, Aunt Myrtle had seen that life consisted of nothing more than lack and abundance—people oscillate between the two extremes throughout their rich but purposeless lives. When she was still a teenager, Aunt Myrtle already knew how to earn a living. With the consent of her parents, she freed herself from the confines of school and threw herself into the public spotlight as a model. She knew that many girls her age were told to wear the season's latest fashion and jewelry and dye their hair into dazzling colors for the camera, but not because they maintained pale, fragile skin and stick-thin figures. Between mass-produced fashion products and the diamond-studded accessories and heels and wigs, there was an empty space that could only be filled by girls who knew how to transform themselves.

Aunt Myrtle's precociousness came from her grandmother, who had been plagued by eye floaters for half her life. Her grandmother would often wake from nightmares in the early hours to a sky punctured by black spots, which drew her into yet another nightmare. She would turn her head and confide in my aunt. "These black holes are everywhere; it's like I'm looking into a hollowed-out beehive." Still young, my aunt could only cover her grandmother's eyes with her thin palms.

Later, when Aunt Myrtle and the other models flaunted themselves on the runway like glossy goods, and all the eyes and cameras below the stage zeroed in on them like an audience of voids trying to suck them into their depths, she was reminded of the tiny, black spots that prevented her grandmother from living a normal life. By then, Aunt Myrtle had learned enough to know what the cameras and the ravenous eyes wanted from her, and she would adapt her postures and expressions accordingly. As she and the outfits she wore fed the cavernous space in those eyes, her runway walk filled the seats of the spacious venues, and the revenue from the runways profited the retail market every season. She never regretted dropping out of school; school was just a place that trained people to fit into various jobs, and she already knew where best to fit herself.

"People misunderstand what it is that models do. They think we're abetting an industry that sells nothing but illusions, that all models do is glue on fake eyelashes and apply artificial color to our skin. In reality, our key purpose is to meet the insatiable needs of all the eyes looking at us without losing ourselves or causing offense." Aunt Myrtle's indignance made me feel that she was talking about a part of herself she sorely missed, but then she carried on, saying that the first skill models learn is the same as people recovering from separation surgery—not to stand or walk but to fall, and how to pick yourself up from the ground.

When Aunt Myrtle collapsed on the runway for the first time, she didn't bleed or get hurt, though she heard an unmistakable snicker. Sitting up on the wooden stage, she was confronted by eyes honing in on her like never before, sharp and searing like light refracted off the waves when the sun is about to set. In that sea of eyes, only one pair looked at her without judgment. She thought she could see herself in them, before realizing that she was staring at her own reflection in two flat lenses. Below those lenses was a pair of thin, stiff lips. The man was wearing a light blue suit that looked too tight on him, as was fashionable at the time. She stood back up on the runway as if nothing had happened, limped through the stream of bodies strutting forward, and went backstage.

Once there, she spaced out in front of the mirror like an unmoving block of ice, and it was like she was in a trance for days until she noticed lattices of rain all over the window, the weight of the raindrops tapping on the glass helping her attune to a clear voice inside of her. In the past, she'd always thought that she was the perfect filler for the apparel and accessories she modeled, but that rainy morning, she knew that something solid inside of her was slowly melting, exposing pinprick holes that she'd kept hidden deep within herself. She saw her reflection in the window and was surprised to find that she looked as porous as a lotus root. She was reminded of the group of girls she worked with, each of whom had their own addictions: shopping, excessive handwashing, drugs, lovers, abuse, gambling, alcohol, a combination of a few of these, as if to instill themselves with some kind of strength. Aunt Myrtle could no longer look down on them as she had before. In fact, she had become one of them, and with affinity came the safety of being around people of the same mind.

The man in the glasses snuck backstage and ran up to my aunt after she'd already removed her vibrant makeup and appeared even more frail and helpless. Gasping, he told her he'd recently stopped smoking. "See, my teeth are pearly white," he said, flashing Aunt Myrtle, young and bewildered, a toothy grin.

From that day onward, Aunt Myrtle no longer went straight back to her solitary room after work. She'd thought she could only relax in cheap, cramped hotel rooms, but the man showed her that she enjoyed going to bars and restaurants and sitting on terraces overlooking the sea, where they exchanged so many words of no consequence. Years later, she would completely forget their conversations, remembering only his encompassing gaze, which seemed to stretch from one end of the horizon to the other, and the way she sunk completely into his depths until she was brimming with abundance. They wandered the streets till late at night, often in silence, swelling like the high tide.

Even immersed in great joy, Aunt Myrtle could still feel that the important parts of herself were being forcefully cut off, like the moments when she sat and cried to herself in the dark, or when she relished a bowl of instant noodles—the solitude and joy that came with freedom had been chased away by his shadow, turning her into a husk of herself. Paradoxically, the gaze he held her in also gave her the courage to face the crowd, injecting her bony legs with a kind of vitality that made her more enthusiastic than usual about her shows. The wide, haphazard eyes gaping at her from below the stage no longer looked like flowers or jellyfish waiting to eat her alive—they just reminded her of the man with glasses.

"In all likelihood, we were codependent and spiraling toward our downfall, but neither of us was willing to admit it," Aunt Myrtle said, sitting across from me, while I remained noncommittal.

When the man with glasses proposed conjoining, Aunt Myrtle thought it was a natural conclusion—after all, there weren't many paths for them to choose from. But although they still looked intoxicated by each other, their smiles would go stale once they noticed the persistent insects in the fast-food restaurants they frequented, the food scraps stuck on the bar carpets, or when they got sick of the humidity by the seaside. Aunt Myrtle was also clearly aware that modeling was a short career; even if she kept herself as thin as possible, she would still be discarded once models who could serve as better filler were hired. For her and the man with glasses to keep moving forward, they must have a goal, some sort of mirage in the far distance.

"Nothing was more aspirational than the dream of conjoinment. It seemed so tangible, it made us think there were still good things in life," my aunt said, as if to mock herself.

They were quick and assertive in signing their consent forms and chose to each amputate an arm to join at the shoulder. She decided to cut off her left arm while he, driven by chivalric compulsion, offered to forego his right arm. But on that day, he started smoking again; in fact he smoked more than ever before, and often brooded with an unreadable look of trepidation on his face. She saw his decline like a new side of him, an excrescence from deep within his soul, but he reassured her, saying that he was only training the dexterity of his left hand.

The doctor and the lawyer overseeing their conjoinment gave them encouragement, saying how Aunt Myrtle and the man with glasses weren't losing an arm, but gaining an extra body, and that once they coordinated with each other, they would become more efficient at all the things they did. The pair had sounded so sincere, Aunt Myrtle couldn't help but believe them, and with this promising sense of their new form, she and the man with glasses started their conjoined life together. But the abrupt change in physical distance caused them to trip, made them step on and kick each other's heels until they bled, and once she could no longer bear the escalating pain, she began to have recurring dreams of escape. One time, when he was fast asleep, she withdrew a butcher knife from the drawer, angled the blade to the place where they were joined, and was about to swing it down—then the words of the doctor and the lawyer flooded her mind with guilt and made her put that rusty knife away.

Aunt Myrtle had no way of knowing what the man with glasses was thinking. Once their wound healed, they worked closely together and tended to matters of life like they were born partners, but they never talked deeply with each other ever again. Conversation had become laborious, which she attributed to some surgical error. "They misjudged the impact distance has on us. Our proximity only accelerated our boredom with each other." After the operation, they couldn't look each other in the eye, and if they tried to look at the other person's face, everything was blurry and out of focus, so they could no longer see the changes in expression or tell what the other person was feeling. Yet, as with countless other things in life that were difficult to accept, they just lived with it, and their days continued on. They fell further into silence as they resented the presence of the body next to them, and sometimes even turned their heads away for some fresh air.

She once had this idea that the man attached to her wasn't the same person she'd chosen to be with. "This must be the mistake of some overworked doctor, who sewed me to the wrong man in a state of confusion." She was thinking about the medical incidents that often happened, and described them in dramatic detail to her conjoined relatives and friends. She'd thought that her speculation would resonate with these people, but they only stared at her with pity in their eyes as they gave her solemn advice. "Suspicion will destroy your life," they said, making her feel like she'd fallen into a trap in the snow, a place so desolate, no one would hear her even if she screamed her throat raw. Not only did the people she spoke to turn a blind eye to her sorrow, the man with glasses, witnessing all of this, also just smoked in silence, his head turned to the side.

She had to think of some other way to escape. *Either I kill him or I kill myself, then at least one of us can break away from this body and live a new life.* But just as she was finished gathering medicine and a gleaming knife and had hidden them in the bedroom drawer, the social worker, who regularly checked on them, and her older sister found out about her plan. When they discovered the brown bottle she'd stored the pills in and turned to scrutinize her, they talked so gently, it made her heart shiver. "This isn't the right way to deal with the problem. You're still immature."

A formidable array of visitors also streamed into the apartment. As one of the women started speaking, another woman echoed her words in support: "Most of the people who can't adapt to conjoined life have a tendency to dissociate from reality. They drown in their own fantasies, forgetting that a conjoined couple is still made up of two distinct bodies who grow and age in different ways. Your priority now is to adjust your pace to the same speed."

Another young woman chirped haughtily to educate my aunt: "Conjoinment is a lifelong game; there's no need to take it so seriously."

In the end, Aunt Myrtle was left standing with her arm hanging by her side in the corridor of the apartment, like a student who had violated the school rules. The man with glasses stood next to her in the same position but with a sneer on his face, as if this was a matter that didn't concern him. They watched as the group of women (and the partners they were conjoined with, who stayed silent the entire time) ransacked their place with practiced ease and collected all the pill bottles and any object they construed to be a weapon. When the crowd left, Aunt Myrtle pulled the man with glasses to the kitchen to stand before their emptied cabinets, and was overcome with shame and remorse. She agreed with what the women had said; she despised the part of her that continued to refuse conjoinment.

For the next fifteen years, Aunt Myrtle wavered between two opposing mindsets. Sometimes, she couldn't ignore the growing clusters of holes within her, which left her with a desperate need to be filled, and as the emotional bridge connecting her and the man with glasses had already been severed, she kept yearning to escape from their shell of a union. Other times, she was determined to do everything she could to be an exemplary partner.

"Why weren't you content with the role you played, instead allowing yourself to be so madly divided?" I couldn't help but ask, and was surprised how aggressive the words sounded when they slipped out of my mouth.

"Because it wasn't something that came from my mind." Aunt Myrtle leaned on the couch, her posture reminding me of a tree blown down by the wind. She continued emphatically, "Those words of discontent and reproach that were directed at me in my head actually belonged to somebody else, or were rules laid down by other people. I mistook them to be my own thoughts, that they must be right." After fifteen years passed, she realized the resentment she'd accumulated in a corner inside of her had hardly diminished, growing into an unmanageable mass, and she finally made up her mind to eradicate it from her body.

"The resentment wasn't directed at anyone. It could be him, or my friends who succumbed to conjoinment, the doctor, the lawyer, anybody on the street, or maybe just myself," she said. At the time, the only thing she was sure of was that she and the man with glasses needed to separate, even if what lay ahead of her was a life without an arm or an identity. Her empty left sleeve would be a reminder that she must amputate parts that didn't belong to her in order to live as a fuller person.

"The separation wasn't a difficult decision," my aunt said, with a conviction that seemed to offer reassurance.

"To some, separation surgery is a part of conjoinment, a phase we must go through." When she told the man with glasses that she was going to take back her half of the body, he dazed for a moment like he had short-circuited, but soon a weak smile returned to his face, and he said, "We'll do whatever you say." For all the years of their conjoinment, these were the same words he would say every time they decided to throw out bulky furniture or change the flooring. A familiar anger rose and smothered her from all sides. By saying those words, he was passing all the decision-making to her, so she would be the only one to bear responsibility for the consequences. She felt rage, and with it, inarticulable loneliness—like a withering branch in the biting winter wind, lashing back and forth until she was about to snap.

Much like the surgery that had connected their bodies, the operation to separate them went surprisingly smooth. Everything was just as the black-market doctor promised, and for that, Aunt Myrtle was vaguely disappointed. To cut back on costs and delays in public hospitals, they'd decided to do the operation in a shop next to a frozen meat stall in an old wet market on a weekend morning. It was run by a man wearing a blue sweatshirt, who'd fled from the north to the city ten years ago with a medical license that wasn't recognized here. To make ends meet, he worked as a butcher, using his skill at dissecting human bodies on pigs and cows. No other job played to his talents as much as working in a meat stall. But one day, when he was cleaning the slaughterhouse, the thought that he would never get to practice as a doctor again came to him and made him take off his apron. A week later, he rented the nearby store space, which had been left vacant for a long time, so that he could "work in the shadows," or so he said. With his reputation and connections, more people came to his clinic than the pigs he'd butchered at the market. As time went by, blue pooled in the shadows of his eyes, but in exchange, he earned himself a skilled pair of hands.

After the black-market doctor recounted his experience to Aunt Myrtle and the man with glasses, he observed their faces in succession and said that all of his patients had been happy with the wounds he sutured, like he was trying to calm their nervous, trembling bodies—it was much easier to inject anesthetics when there was less tension in the muscles.

Aunt Myrtle lay on the operating table, knowing that it was the last time in their lives that she and the man would be conjoined. Her consciousness fogged as she waited for her own butchering, and she couldn't tell if she was a sheep, a pig, a cow, a chicken, or a human being; it seemed like she could be anything or nothing at all.

"When I woke up, he was lying on another bed. It was an unbelievable sight." Many years had passed, but Aunt Myrtle still remembered his emaciated body, like a deflated ball. It was then that she realized his aversion to words was perhaps to avoid revealing any hint of pain, and that the qualities that had made him special were somehow lost little by little over the years, the way air seeps from a ball as time passes. She could think of no other reason than it being the natural order of things.

Before they were allowed to return to their homes, the black-market doctor asked them to stay at the clinic for monitoring until they'd gotten past the dangerous postoperative period. In the sealed room, the man became her only window. With nothing else to do throughout the day, she cast her eyes on his flaccid torso, and felt a certain thread of their connection stir once more.

"After we left that clinic, we never saw each other again. I even lost his contact info, but there's always something that links us together, like the matching scars on our bodies, or the way we'd gotten used to sitting when we were conjoined."

By the time my aunt finished pouring out her story, the sky outside the window was a wash of blue-black, a canopy about to fall onto the building, draping across this entire district that was going to be forgotten. I was coming up with the words to say goodbye, but then my aunt spoke again, her voice full of sorrow as she said she could never forgive the man with glasses for refusing to accept her left arm as a parting gift. After their conjoinment surgery, the doctor had given back her severed left arm in a clear plastic bag, which she'd embalmed like an animal specimen and stored in a rectangular box.

"He said he wouldn't take it because he couldn't possibly look after my stiff arm; the responsibility was too much for him," she complained. Then she asked if I wanted to see it, like she was seeking consolation for the neglect she'd held close to her heart. "Honestly, it looks just like a polished piece of wood," she added with a shrug.

I didn't have it in me to reject her, so I nodded. I watched as she stood, her hand holding the walls and furniture as she limped into her room. When her silhouette melted into the shadows at the end of the corridor, I mustered as much strength as I could to support my and Lok's bodies and stepped through the door, away from that slanted building.

Sitting in the car and looking back at the building through the window, I realized how much it looked like a ship that was about to sink. The look in my aunt's eyes as she told her story lingered in my mind. It proved to me that she never recognized me and just thought I was a new client coming in for a consultation, and I was given the pleasure of glimpsing her secrets without being discovered.

Case Study II

Death Carnival: Evelyn Fisherman / Josephine Fisherman

Hardly anyone believed the harrowing tale of the lake in Third Face Memorial Park, which explained why the park was still so crowded on holidays and weekends. People didn't go there for strolls, but to reach the lake's edge so they could kneel and stare at their reflections in the water. They would wait for the wind to blow, the fish to swim by, or a sudden rain to break the surface, so they could see their faces splinter into fragments that stretched and spread unceasingly with the ripples.

In a rumor about the park, if you leaned close enough to the water right at that moment, you would catch a glimpse of your true inner self. People had taken it to be a marketing strategy to attract tourists, which was why they still went to the lake on holidays to peer into the water for fun or as a kind of experiment. From early morning, people would line up outside the gates of the park for a ticket. They took turns heading to the edge of the lake, bending down and encircling the shore with a thicket of bodies, while the people waiting wandered around to stretch their legs.

The first person to perish in the water after sitting by the lake and staring at their own reflection was Evelyn. When Evelyn jumped and drowned herself, the park was still semi-abandoned; there were barely any visitors, and the lake was a foul pool clogged with mud, industrial waste from factories, and garbage and food scraps from nearby residences. Evelyn allegedly sank to the bottom, but the rescue workers never located her body. After much fanfare and coverage in the press, the city planners, in an effort to divert people's attention from the incident and also drive away the park's homeless population, set aside a budget to renovate the area and renamed it Third Face Memorial Park. No one knew whose third face it was, if it belonged to each of the city's residents or Evelyn.

As the city's first conjoined person to undergo a successful separation surgery, Evelyn, sitting in a wheelchair, was a symbol of independence and freedom. To

Evelyn, however, she felt she was born incapable of being on her own and was forsaken by life without ever being free. She always turned down media requests, detesting journalists who might invade her privacy, and had only ever been interviewed for *Betrayed Bodies: Conjoinment and the Obstacles of Daily Life* for academic purposes.

In the interview, she said that whenever she ventured outside in her wheelchair, she felt like she was teetering on the brink of the world no matter where she was in the city, about to keel over into the abyss of outer space. There could be no wind, no dust in the air, and still she would feel the stab of a million invisible spikes driving her away to a distance beyond distance. This sensation had been with her ever since she woke from surgery; it seeded in her heart, burgeoned, and grew, until it became her understanding of life and her unbreakable belief about the future.

From birth, Evelyn had been convinced that she wasn't a whole individual, but part of a whole—cog of a colossal machine, thread of a rope, a flower petal. She had always considered herself to be half of "Evelyn and Josephine Fisherman, the conjoined sisters," with both Evelyn and Josephine integral to existence. She never understood Josephine's resolution to separate their bodies, and only submitted to her sister's wishes.

She recounted the moment when she woke up from the anesthetic: she was in a room, and when she saw she was the only person in it, she immediately knew she had been the only one to survive the surgery. She wasn't surprised at all that at least one of them would die during the operation, but it took her a long time to recover from the shock that they hadn't died together and she, not Josephine, had been the one to live. This was the only deviation from the doctors' prognosis, for Josephine, being physically stronger, should have had a better chance of survival. The rest of the operation went largely as expected. After the separation, without the support and balance of her other half, she would never be able to walk again.

"Josephine said we could make wheelchairs or crutches our new support to help maneuver our changed bodies." According to Evelyn, Josephine had been impervious to the repercussions of surgery. Compared to separating their bodies, all other things, including the life of her own sister, seemed to be of little importance. Once Evelyn saw the determination on Josephine's face, she found her sister as unfamiliar and distant as the lone passersby on the streets, who were all set in their freedom, walking swiftly in solitude. Their parents, doctors, nurses, even reporters and neighbors, people who had never met them before, all looked at them with pity. They saw themselves as saviors, determining that in order for the sisters to lead normal lives, they must cut them off of each other.

"Josephine must have made the decision to separate because she was inundated by these opinions," Evelyn said, and believed her sister had forgotten about the special circumstances that distinguished them from everybody else. "She just hadn't thought it through. Like fish out of water, we never would've survived once we were apart from each other."

To Evelyn, the surgery meant more than her and Josephine's physical separation. Josephine was taking away parts of her body and taking the side of people different than they were. All Evelyn could think about the surgery was how it was going to tear her apart until she was scattered in different places, never to be put back together. Yet she stayed silent while people enthused over the details of the surgery, not to make herself the more docile sister, more willing to listen and submit, but because she clearly understood how terrifying surgeries were—the doctors never had a complete grasp of a patient's needs, any yet most patients could only put their blind faith in their medical reasoning and consent to the methods used to slice their body open. Evelyn knew from the onset that the surgery was going to be a catastrophe, but she still offered her consent.

She said, "Up until the last moment, I'd hoped that I could think like those people, so I tried my best to bend myself to them." But the true reason might have been that Evelyn lacked the courage to voice her thoughts. The only hope she harbored deep within was that she and Josephine would die on the operating table together—that was as close to a happy and achievable outcome as she could imagine.

According to Erich Fromm's psychoanalyst theory, Evelyn had a masochistic character, meaning she would rather surrender her freedom than face the fear of taking control over her solitude. She placed her life in the hands of her sister, parents, and doctors, and forfeited her own volition. But the question is, how is freedom defined? If freedom is the pursuit of one's truest feelings, even if Evelyn's actions went beyond what is commonly understood as free, as long as they were decisions she had consciously made out of her need for attachment, to sacrifice a part of her liberty for a greater liberty, then she was not masochistic in stripping herself of autonomy.

Evelyn's body healed irrevocably against her will after the surgery. She learned to use a wheelchair to get around, but sometimes couldn't help but lose her way—it had always been Josephine who determined which direction they should go. Now, Evelyn had to decide what food she liked instead of matching someone else's taste, pick the color of her clothes, answer questions and accept or reject suggestions. She said that living wasn't painful or difficult, she just had no idea how to do it this way.

What helped her face the troubles of solitary life wasn't medication or words of encouragement, but her death fantasies. People came into her hospital room to check on her healing wound and, more importantly, to see for themselves that she had indeed survived. When Evelyn saw their ecstatic expressions, as if they were witnessing some sort of miracle, she understood her body was no longer her own, caught between a death wish and guilt at the thought of disappointing those countless faces she saw. Still, when she imagined her body dispersing into the air as countless particles, the elation was like morphine for her sorrows. She told her interviewer that everyone is dying on a daily basis, it is how we connect and fuse with the world: through our fallen hair that clumps with dust, flakes of skin dropped on the floor or washed down the drain, oils absorbed by bedsheets and clothes, feces that becomes fertilizer for gardens.

"People just never notice," she said.

No one could tell exactly what happened to Evelyn that day. The only eyewitness—walking through the park to his apartment building, holding a basket of groceries—glimpsed a dark, thin shadow fall out of a wheelchair into the lake like a piece of clothing blown off a railing. When he ran to the shore, there was nothing but the wheelchair, seat still slightly warm, the wavering water, and his own reflection.

Evelyn's parents held a funeral for her, but it was more like a carnival, per Evelyn's wishes, and no one could verify if the incident was a mishap or an end that she chose. There wasn't a dress code for guests to follow, only instructions for the expressions they could wear: maniacal laughter, endless tears, or a face like an impassive pile of ash. Her parents felt these were the only appropriate ways for people to show their feelings about losing Evelyn.

The park was closed for a while. When it reopened, the lake had been thoroughly dredged and looked as polished as a mirror. According to a survey conducted by a university in 2002, those who were curious visited the lake at first to see Evelyn's spirit, rumored to inhabit the bottom of the lake. About eighty percent of the respondents said that when they looked into the water, they found it so exceptionally pellucid, their reflections were clearer and more defined than in any mirror they had ever seen. Even when their faces were ripped into pieces by the waves, they still felt like they had gained enough strength from the experience to return to the drudgery of their lives.

Specimen

"Did everything go well?" Lok asked as soon as he woke up. To show my appreciation for his patience, I nodded enthusiastically. He gave me a smile that was as bright and naive as a child's, which made my heart lurch in fear.

That night, I sat with him before our two-person desk. While sorting his patient files, he said to me, his tone buoyant like a song, that once I finished the dissertation I'd dragged on forever, we could put all our energy into his clinic and expand the business until everyone thought of him and the music he played on sleepless nights. I could feel his heartbeat through the skin of my chest; it once troubled me to no end but had become a daily rhythm. As I wrote about my aunt's case on my laptop, I imagined how he would react when he woke up and found out I was missing from his body. There might be a hole in his chest, where he would feel a draft, and so, to minimize his discomfort, I decided to leave him a larger piece of muscle for the doctors to trim. He continued to speak and gestured like he was performing a virtuosic piece, and I envisioned the hole in his chest expanding viciously and turning hideous. I spread my body and extended my limbs as far as they would go, but I couldn't fill it up.

◡

Once Lok closed his eyes to sleep, my time alone officially began. It was going to be a busy day: I needed to set my plan in motion and bring everything to a close before the sky turned dark. I was to deliver a copy of my dissertation to Professor Foot's office at the scheduled time, and soon, everything would be over.

I threw all my personal belongings in the apartment, my books, clothes, everything that I owned, into a black plastic bag to save Lok the trouble of cleaning up after me. It was an arduous task with Lok's sleeping form weighing down half of my body. As I cleaned, I wrestled with his weight, and was fortunate to emerge victorious. The only thing that gave me pause was a brown piece of hemp rope, long enough to encircle the perimeter of the apartment. I once thought of it as a coiled snake in the closet, but looking at it again now, it was more like a severed tail. I couldn't possibly throw it out with the rest of my things, so I put it in a leather bag and dialed Bak's number.

His voice was cool metal, like before, but he was never the type to refuse a request.

I told him that my dissertation had reached its final stage. To verify my data, it was necessary for me to understand the recent condition of each subject and determine if amendments should be made to the research. "It'll be a short meeting," I said.

He hesitated for a moment, then proposed to meet at a motel. "I have another person's weight on my shoulders now; it's a burden no matter how you look at it." He said he could barely walk, and relied on vehicles to get around. His voice was laced with inexplicable excitement.

"It's the same for me," I said. "The person I'm with weighs more than I do."

When I opened the door to the motel room, Bak was already sitting on the couch. We had both come with our burdens, so we weren't able to lend a helping hand to each other. To prevent the sleeping Lok from getting injured or toppling over, I staggered and dragged him to lie on the mattress, then I greeted Bak, asking how he was. A quiet, gentle smile spread across his face, which I'd remembered to be stony and impassive. My eyes drifted to the person extending from his chest. Like Lok, she was asleep, the corners of her mouth curled upward like a cat in its dreams. I thought, for no apparent reason, that she was a part Bak had always harbored, or Bak was bringing out a previously unknown side of her, or maybe both were true. Side by side, they looked like trees in the winter, bare of leaves and flowers, so dense and intertwined it was impossible to tell bough from branch. Her body was smaller than his, so he cradled her in his arms like a child.

I dug out the bundle of rope from my leather bag and tossed it to him. He held the rope and carefully examined it, then looked at me in confusion.

"Tie this between the two of you," I said. In the eighteenth century, parents who gave birth to conjoined children were often unable to come to terms with reality and reacted to the brutal surprise in various ways. Some tied a rope around the flesh where the infants were connected in an attempt to separate them.

"But we have no intention of cutting each other away from our bodies," he protested.

"You can't separate people with rope," I said. "This is a ritual that does the opposite."

He hesitated for a moment, but finally made an

intricate knot around the muscles joining their bodies, then he hastily untied it.

"That's it." I said, and I let out a breath.

He returned the rope to me, then he gave me a nod and left, carefully holding his partner in his arms and closing the door behind him. I heard his footsteps tread down the carpeted corridor, followed by the start of a car engine, and them driving away. Only then did I lift Lok back up, feeling every bit of his weight and pressure on me.

It was almost evening by the time my taxi drove toward Professor Foot's academic building. The streets were filled with people heading home—people who were conjoined, single, with parts of their bodies missing, walking toward me from the distance and flitting by before receding to other places. I took out a glass bottle and swallowed all the pills inside. The pills were as colorful as candy and would take me to the place I needed to be.

When I reached Professor Foot's office, books, papers, an undistinguishable clutter of things, were stacked in front of his desk like hills with different shapes and peaks, shielding his face from view. As I heaved Lok across the room, I ran into more obstacles than I anticipated, so it was only when I stumbled close that I saw the shock of gray hair on the professor's head. But the long crinkles of crow's feet around his eyes enlivened his face, making him appear almost approachable.

He looked up at me, and for a moment he was stupefied. "Why are you carrying such heavy luggage?" he asked, pointing at Lok, who was in his sleeping bag.

"Because I'm going away on a trip," I said, joking, though I had no way of knowing if he understood what I was implying. I quickly changed the subject. "Are you busy?"

"Not really." He shrugged and put his one leg on the table. "It's all work that won't amount to anything." Following that, words flowed from his mouth like he was reciting lines from a poem: "We step into classrooms to end the semester, propose theses to abandon research, and graduate to face the prospect of unemployment. At long last, people, students and teachers, leave this place one after the other, until we can no longer call it a school." His eyes glinted with excitement.

I carried on his train of thought: "We are born to die in abundance, and mend our bodies so we can cut them open." I took out a bound copy of my dissertation from my leather bag and placed it in his hands. The weighty stack of paper had finally left me; I could feel my body become light as a wisp.

"That's the textual component of my dissertation."
With Lok in tow, I squeezed into a crevice among the mess
of the desk, books, and other things and lay down. "As for
my field research, I'll need your help to complete it."

"What do you mean?"

Foot's voice sounded like it came from distant clouds.
He made a low gasp as he tripped over his piles of books.
Eventually his face appeared right before my eyes. He lowered his head and looked at me, his expression frozen like
the work of some stiff actor. It was a completely unfamiliar reaction, a part of himself that he'd kept hidden, now
suddenly exposed. I couldn't help but revel in his loss of
composure, and then the world before me fell apart. The
drugs were starting to take effect. I knew.

"Before I stop breathing." I wanted to tell him that
he was to take me to the hospital, separate Lok from my
body, and disseminate the parts of me following the instructions in the appendix of my paper. That he should
hurry because Lok was in danger of dying. But my tongue
had already gone numb and swollen, and I lost the ability
to speak clearly.

"This is a joke." Professor Foot's voice was stern and
hoarse, as if giving an order.

I tried my best to look him in the eye, but my vision

was tumultuous as my organs churned, slow and then quicker, quicker, soon surging so violently that they were about to spill out from my throat. Before I had time to react, the waves rose within me and engulfed my voice completely.

Professor Foot's head hovered above me, surrounded by a thin ring of light. It was like I'd fallen into a well, but instead of plummeting, I was floating in all directions, moving rapidly with the wind and flying away.

Later, in the operating room. My heart was cut out and transplanted into a woman's body. My right arm was preserved and sent to my aunt, who paired it with her left arm and put them in a blue brocade box with desiccants. My hair was tied into a bundle with a ribbon like a present and sent to Bak, who examined it for a second before throwing it into the depths of a drawer, then forgot to take it with him when he moved. Professor Foot was given one of my legs, which he made into a specimen and displayed in his office, sometimes joking with students that he had exchanged his leg for another person's. I left the muscles around my chest for Lok, but most of them were chopped off by the surgeon performing our separation and thrown out with other surgical waste. The remaining bones and flesh, steeped in a bottle of tea-colored solution, were given to my mother. Whenever her relatives and friends visited, saw the bottle, and gave their polite condolences, my mother would sigh and say, "It's better to have a boy if you want children. Boys are stronger—have a daughter, and this is all that's going to be left of her."

As time went on, the sorrow in her sighs waned and turned hollow, joining the daily hum of her home.

HON LAI CHU is one of Hong Kong's most prominent writers, and the author of several novels, including *Mending Bodies*, *Degravitation Zone*, and *A Dictionary of Two Cities*, co-authored with Dorothy Tse, which won the Hong Kong Book Prize. Her most recent works include *Half-Eclipse* and *Darkness under the Sun*, two diaristic essay collections about Hong Kong and the pandemic. She has also received accolades from Taiwan's Unitas Literary Association, the Shih-Chiu Liang Literature Award, the Dream of the Red Chamber Award, and the Hong Kong Biennial Awards for Chinese Literature, among many others.

JACQUELINE LEUNG is a writer and translator from Hong Kong. Her work has appeared or is forthcoming in *Wasafiri*, *Transtext(e)s Transcultures*, *Gulf Coast*, *Asymptote*, *Nashville Review*, *SAND Journal*, the *Asian Review of Books*, *Cha*, *Books From Taiwan*, and elsewhere. She is a translation editor at *The Offing*, Asian Cultural Council's 2024/2025 New York Fellow, and previously managed the Hong Kong International Literary Festival. Her excerpt of *Mending Bodies* was a winner of PEN Presents. This is her first full-length translation.

Printed in the USA
CPSIA information can be obtained
at www.ICGtesting.com
CBHW052303021124
16701CB00008B/82

2 370001 947306